KISSING TED CALLAHAN

(and other guys)

KISSING TED CALLAHAN

(and other guys)

AMY SPALDING

poppy

Little, Brown and Company

New York   Boston

Poppy

Hachette Book Group
1290 Avenue of the Americas, New York, NY 10104
Visit us at lb-teens.com

Poppy is an imprint of Little, Brown and Company.
The Poppy name and logo are trademarks of Hachette Book Group, Inc.

"Everything" © 2014 Nadia Osman. Lyrics written by Nadia Osman.

The publisher is not responsible for websites (or their content) that are not owned by the publisher.

First Edition: April 2015

Library of Congress Cataloging-in-Publication Data

Spalding, Amy.
Kissing Ted Callahan (and other guys) : a novel / by Amy Spalding. — First edition.
pages cm
Summary: Sixteen-year-olds Riley and Reid make a pact to pursue their respective crushes and document the experiences in a shared notebook they call "The Passenger Manifest."
ISBN 978-0-316-37152-0 (hardcover) — ISBN 978-0-316-37151-3 (ebook) — ISBN 978-0-316-37150-6 (library edition ebook) [1. Dating (Social customs)— Fiction. 2. Friendship—Fiction.] I. Title.
PZ7.S73189Ki 2015 [Fic]—dc23 2014015563

10 9 8 7 6 5 4 3 2 1

RRD-C

Printed in the United States of America

To my friend Todd Martens

Sound is the love between me and you.

—Wild Flag, "Romance"

TWO MONTHS AGO

"This summer is a failure."

"Reid, get a grip," I say.

"It's emblematic," he says, and I don't roll my eyes because Reid says things like *emblematic* all the time. He's a writer, but also he's just Like That. "This is the summer before our junior year, and it isn't going how I wanted."

"It's one sold-out show," I say.

We didn't buy tickets to see Welcome to the Marina in advance because even our bandmates, Lucy and Nathan, said their record wasn't very good, and *Pitchfork* said they were even worse live. But as soon as we drove up to the Center for the Arts Eagle Rock and saw the line wrapping around the entrance and stairs, we realized we should have just ponied up the extra money for the Ticketmaster fees and bought tickets in advance. "What should we do now? Pastrami and shakes at the Oinkster?"

"I'm too disappointed for a pastrami sandwich," Reid says.

"Let's just go back to the garage and see if Lucy and Nathan want to practice more."

This seems like a good solution, even though I'd really been hoping for one of the Oinkster's ube shakes. Today's had been one of those band practices where, if not for Reid and I having plans, we could have played all night.

I love being in a band with people who care about it as much as I do.

We shout-sing along with Andrew Mothereffing Jackson's latest album on the drive back and pull up to Lucy's house less than an hour after we left it. Nathan's car is still there, so we made the right call.

"You guys were wrong," I say as Reid opens the door to the garage. "That show is completely sold out."

A Crocodiles song is blaring from the stereo, but somehow the room still seems completely silent because no one is talking. I see it like a horror movie, all quick flashes of skin and slo-mo devastation. Nathan is on Lucy, or maybe Lucy is on Nathan, but regardless of who is on whom, it's Lucy and Nathan. Lucyandnathan.

Now everything's in fast-forward instead. Lucy and Nathan are fully dressed and talking at exactly the same time, but Reid and I might as well be turned into stone.

"We wanted to tell you guys," I hear Nathan say.

"We were *going* to tell you," I hear Lucy say.

"Nothing changes about the band."

2

"*Yes.* Everything will be exactly the same."

Reid and I manage to break our stone spell at the same moment. I know if I wanted to, I could speak again. But all we do is back out of the garage together and get into Reid's car without another word.

CHAPTER ONE

We, the undersigned, agree to document our journeys in search of true love and/or sex. No detail is too small, too humiliating, too stupid.

We will also provide one another with advice on how to capture the attention of the opposite gender. No line items should be taken as criticism, merely assistance and guidance to complete our ultimate goal.

Signed:

Riley Jean Crowe-Ellerman
Reid Daniel Goodwin

CHAPTER TWO

Ted Callahan is walking to my car.

I am trying to act normal. Like a normal person. Pick up one foot, put it down, repeat with the other foot. Do not look like a robot while doing so. Do not tip over. Do not, under any circumstances, let out any joyous squeals. Do not grab Ted's face and scream, "Dear god, you are here and you are real and you are beautiful and you are about to get into my car."

"Thanks," Ted says.

I've been in love with him for at least five months, but he doesn't talk to me often. His words are blue sky, cutting through the clouds of our previously uncommunicative ways.

"It's no problem. I drive this way anyway." It's scary how fast this flies out of me. Stop talking, Riley. "And I never mind driving. I *love* driving. Ever since I got my license, it's all, if I can get in the car and go, I totally will."

Why did I say that? It isn't even true! I neither love nor hate driving.

Ted nods politely as I unlock the doors to my car. It's as

he's about to sit down that I realize something horrifying—way worse than my stream-of-consciousness ode to the open road—is about to occur. When I dropped off Ashley at school this morning, she left behind her copy of... *Gill Talk*.

On the front passenger seat.

Faceup.

The cover features a pale mermaid with flowing blond locks. Instead of the traditional shell bra, she's wearing a gold shirt that looks like it was purchased at Forever 21, and instead of scales, she appears to possess sequins.

"That isn't mine." I chuck it into the backseat. "I wouldn't read that. It's awful, right? Oh my god, it's so awful."

Ted smiles, but it's like when you're in a terrible situation, such as getting your legs blown off in the war, and you have to pretend for the sake of the children or the elderly that things are actually totally fine, except your crappy fake smile is fooling no one, Ted. Ted! Don't think I'm a weirdo who reads books about teenage mermaids making out with each other.

"I didn't even notice," he says.

"It's so embarrassing." My mouth now works independently of my brain. Or I have some new, secondary brain whose only function is to make boys think I'm stupid. Apparently, this new brain was raised on a diet of bad teen movies and CW dramas. Brain Number Two, I hate you. "One time my sister left that book in this deli, and she didn't realize until later, so I had to go back and ask this old man who runs it if I could have it back. And he doesn't know it's my sister's! So now he thinks I read books that have sparkly people with fins for feet making out on the cover."

Ted fidgets with the zipper on his bag. "Probably he didn't notice."

Then he changes the subject. "What kind of car is this?"

I'm not sure what to make of the question. I do not drive a cool car, and I do not drive a crappy car. I drive Mom's hand-me-down, very normal and nondescript. It's a little dark outside, but he could have figured it out just by walking up to it and getting inside.

Oh! Maybe he's trying to make conversation with me?

"A white 2009 Toyota Corolla." Years pass before the way-too-many words leave my mouth. And why did I say that it was white? The one thing about the car that doesn't need any clarifying is its color.

Ted nods, and I am sure this thing where we exchange words that I can't quite—even being generous—call a conversation is ending. I'm also already turning into the parking lot next to his mom's office building. After Yearbook, when I made this magic happen by offering him a ride, I'd asked him where he was heading. But supertruthfully? I already knew. I spotted him walking here last week.

"Thanks for the ride." He gets out of the car. Swiftly. Too swiftly? Is he afraid I'll lob more word fits at him? Ted, come back! Ted, I'll learn to be normal! Ted, it isn't fair we sat two feet apart and I didn't get to touch your hair!

"Anytime," I say. "Seriously, I don't mind."

"Cool." He picks up his messenger bag and slides it over his shoulder. I admire boys who basically carry purses. They aren't afraid of what the world thinks. "See you, Riley."

"See you."

He walks off toward the building. I wait for it, a glance back. A glance back would hold so much meaning and potential and material for analysis. But Ted walks toward the big glass doors, tries one, and when it's clearly the wrong side, opens the other and disappears inside.

I plug in my earphones and reach for my phone. I saw Reid when school let out at three, but so much has changed since then.

"The plan is doomed." I know it sounds overdramatic, but I also know it isn't. Not at all. "Ted was in my car."

"Ted? Ted Callahan?" His voice washes over with realization. "Ted Callahan is the Crush?"

"TED CALLAHAN IS THE CRUSH." I sound insane. Brain Number Two seems to be planning an overthrow.

"We'll meet up." Reid is all business. Often, it's what I like most about him. "The usual? Now?"

"Now."

CHAPTER THREE

Reid's Goals (in Order):

1. Flirting
2. Chemistry
3. Hanging out
4. Dates
5. Making out
6. Love
7. Commitment
8. Sex

Riley's Goals (in Order):

1. Witty/sexy banter
2. Listening to music/going to shows together
3. Doing it!!

CHAPTER FOUR

There used to be four. Lucy and Reid and Nathan and me. Against the world. Well, not the world. Not really against anything.

Lucy and I have been best friends since we were five and stood next to each other in Beginners Tap. Reid went to our school and had since kindergarten. He'd seemed like kind of a dork for a long time, but he sat behind us in freshman English, and he made great jokes about the ancient stuff we were forced to read. More importantly, his taste in music was excellent, though sometimes he could make even *that* dorky, like by geeking out over original vinyl pressings. Still, once we found out the battered Moleskine notebooks he was never seen without were filled with lyrics—and really smart and funny and heartbreaky lyrics at that—I knew for sure I wanted him around.

Back then Nathan rolled with a preppier and more athletically inclined crowd, but some mutual acquaintance told him we should talk about music, since we often ended up at school wearing the same band T-shirts. And then everything started happening.

The four of us listened to music, and then played music, and then wrote music. About a year and a half ago, we started calling ourselves a band—the Gold Diggers—and then Nathan's cousin booked us to be the opener at his wedding. (Yes, apparently some weddings have multiple bands play— especially if one of those bands is made up of a cousin you feel bad for and his friends.)

It was actually as easy and awesome as it sounds.

Last summer, Lucy's dad let us convert their garage into rehearsal space, I saved enough Christmas and birthday money to upgrade my drum kit, Reid let Lucy and me take him shopping so he'd stop dressing like his mom picked out his clothes (she did), and Nathan designed a band logo and found us two more gigs. Things were Happening. I walked around in the kind of mood where I wanted to high-five people and shout about how great life was.

But then the Incident happened.

Reid and I have talked about it a lot since. Not, like, in graphic detail. But things have shifted. We don't know what our group is anymore, even though Nathan and Lucy say "It's just the same!" while holding hands and whispering into each other's ears and sliding into the booth side of our usual table at Palermo Pizza while Reid and I get stuck in the rickety chairs facing them.

And permanent relocation to rickety chairs is definitely *not just the same.*

* * *

"Yo." Reid slides in across from me in our new usual spot at Fred 62, which has become our place. It's a diner with old-fashioned orange-and-brown booths and a menu that stretches on for years. It's open twenty-four hours, so it's just as good after concerts as it is after school or band practice.

Maybe I'm just suspicious, but Reid looks smirky. Self-satisfied. Knowledgeable of Things.

His silence is too much. I must make him talk. "Just say it, Reid."

"Ted Callahan?" Reid asks.

I leap forward and shove my hands over his mouth, which is dumb considering he's already said it, and what I'm doing is way more attention-drawing.

"Ow!"

"You're a wimp."

"I know I'm a wimp." He leans forward to grab my bag. I don't argue because we've determined it's the safest place for the Passenger Manifest. One of Reid's notebooks seemed like the perfect place to start logging our plans and thoughts on helping each other in our quest to find love. Well, Reid wants to find love, and I want to do more than awkwardly kiss a boy outside a ninth-grade dance I didn't even technically go to.

Reid named it the Passenger Manifest because it's some reference from that old TV show *Lost*, and that guy loves hanging on to random factoids.

Anyway, if I trust Reid with all of my boy thoughts, what do I care if he sees my lip gloss or tampons?

"Don't put his name in that," I say. "Or his initials. Everyone will know who I mean by his initials."

"I'm putting his initials," Reid says. "I wrote down *names*. No one but us will see this. And if they do, by his initials people could think it's Tyler Cole or Titus Culliver—"

"Gross," I say. "Who would have a crush on Titus Culliver? Sometimes he leaves his prescription goggles on after gym class—"

"Or Tito Cortez," Reid says.

"I had no idea you had some kind of superpower with initials," I say.

"Yeah, it's amazing I don't have a girlfriend, right?" He isn't joking. I have no idea what will happen if everything we've planned works. Reid's identity seems forged around his lack of a lady friend. It's stupid because Reid is good at lots of things that matter: music, school, crossword puzzles. And, apparently, initials. "Oh, this was the thing in your list in the Passenger Manifest: 'Join a club he's in. Give him a ride,'" he says, pointing to the notebook.

"Yearbook," I say. "Last week I noticed he always walks down Sunset to some office building after our meeting, so I offered to drive him."

Reid props his elbows on the table and puts his hands together like he's an evil dictator taking stock of his newly invaded countries. "Not a bad plan."

"I know it's dumb I like him." I lace my fingers and hold my hands over my face like a mask. "You can say it."

Reid laughs. "Well."

I wait for the list of reasons why it's dumb. I'm not breathtakingly pretty, Ted barely knows who I am, I have no boyfriend experience, and I'm aiming too high right out of the gate.

"He's kind of short," Reid says. "And he makes *me* look cool. You know I'm not cool, Ri, no matter what you and Luce say." Reid makes a couple of strange arm movements, and I realize he's imitating the way Ted moves his hands when he's talking.

I feel like yelling at him, but the resemblance is more than uncanny. I am speechless at how it is the exact opposite of canny.

"He's so awkward."

"What?" A protective sensation rises up within me. I had no idea I'd have to defend Ted, ever. "But he's *gorgeous*. And a genius! He runs the freaking *Fencing Club*, you know." The *Fencing Club* is not, as it sounds, a club for fencing, but an underground blog that used to be an underground newspaper that dates back to 1964, the year our school was founded.

"I know he does," Reid says slowly. "Do you think that makes him cool?"

"Yes?" I stare at Reid. "Do you mean Ted isn't cool?"

"Ted Callahan—"

"STOP USING HIS FULL NAME!" I kick Reid in the knee. My legs aren't freakishly strong, like my arms are from drumming, but it's easy to hurt someone's kneecaps. "He could have some relative here. Or a friend we don't know. *BE CAREFUL.*"

Reid's clearly trying to act as if he isn't wounded from my powerful knee kick. "I'm just saying."

"I'm just saying," I say in my mocking-Reid voice. It sounds like a cartoon chipmunk, so I don't know why it's my go-to for making fun of him. Reid has never sounded like a cartoon chipmunk. "So you're saying Ted is *not* out of my league?"

"I'll be diplomatic," he says, "and leave it at that. Yes."

"You're serious?"

"Riley, you're in a band," he says. "You are a Rock Star. I don't even know if Ted listens to music."

"No, I'm sure Ted listens to music." But the authority I would have made that pronouncement with earlier is gone. "So he isn't cool?"

Reid shakes his head. "He is definitely not cool."

My worldview has shifted. Is it possible I might totally and completely be capable of Getting Ted Callahan?

CHAPTER FIVE

Ways to Get Someone's Attention, by Reid and Riley

1. Say something funny—everyone likes to laugh, except jerks!
2. Appear to be really smart about something, but be careful. Some topics (like knowing everything about <u>Doctor Who</u>) will make you seem like a geek, not a genius.
3. Let the person know you guys have something in common, like you both love Ted Leo and the Pharmacists or Daniel Clowes or Grilled Cheese Night at the Oaks.
4. Have a little mystery—for example, say something intriguing and then make an exit before someone can ask a follow-up question.
5. Look really hot, obviously.

CHAPTER SIX

Looking back, I shouldn't have been so shocked at Nathan and Lucy falling for each other. Together they made sense, sure. That much was easy. But this was *my very best friend in the whole wide world.*

This was *Lucy.*

Things were happening with a boy. With *Nathan.* And my very best friend in the whole wide world hadn't told me anything.

And if Reid and I hadn't walked in on them...maybe she never would have.

I hadn't even known I should have been on the lookout for this stuff. Lucy and I talked lots about the kinds of girls who always had boyfriends. We weren't like them, distracted by kissing and jealousy and birth-control options. That stuff could all wait until college or a national tour—whichever came first—when our band was established and we were Serious Musicians Without Curfews.

Reid clearly felt the same way. He couldn't even talk to girls in class without sweating, after all. And grown-ups always acted like peaking in college was way better than peaking in high school, so we had all the time in the world to worry about it. Sure, there were some rumors about Nathan and assorted girls at assorted parties, but he never brought them up, and I dismissed rumors as rumors.

It wasn't as if I didn't get it. Lucy is the kind of girl who could be a Career Princess at Disneyland if she weren't planning on being a rock-star-slash-sociologist. She has almost black hair and delicate, fair skin. She wears dresses with color-coordinated flats *just because,* and she's tiny in the way people think is cute and not shrimpy. While I'm of perfectly average height and size, next to Lucy I'm this lumbering giant. And even when I'm determined to get up early and put effort into how I look, I basically stick to a uniform of a T-shirt, jeans—on crazy days a jean skirt—and a pair of Vans or Chucks. And I'm great with this! I am who I am, and whatever other lame identity slogans, but sometimes I see pictures of Lucy and me and wonder what guy in his right mind would pick anyone but the princess.

And I can't lie. Before catching him mid-grope with Lucy, I'd wondered what it would be like to kiss Nathan. (It seems from Lucy's frequent glazy expression and regular application of lip gloss, that the answer is *good.*) Nathan is one of those guys who hits all the marks, if charting guys were like bird watching or stamp collecting. He's tall, and he probably works out, and he gets good grades but doesn't seem to take that too seriously.

Still, this wasn't supposed to be the track Lucy and I were on, and so it wasn't just that she didn't tell me, and it wasn't just that it was Nathan. It was that my friend was going against so many things we'd talked about, like our two AM conversations suddenly didn't matter at all.

After the Incident, I considered hooking up with Reid to make things even, but I'm not into Reid, not like that. Reid is cute, but I mean that: *cute*. He's shorter than me, but I'm not short, so maybe that's not a big deal. His hair is better than it used to be, but it's boring brown and fluffy like a baby chick's, and that's not the kind of hair I go for in a guy. Not that that's a deal breaker, but also Reid gets really emotional and worked up over the tiniest incidents—like the time Lucy suggested he buy one big bottle of orange juice instead of two small bottles and he thought we all considered him financially irresponsible.

Plus, from his total disinterest that time my white shirt accidentally got soaked—and everyone could see my bra—I know that Reid doesn't want to hook up with me, either. And while I don't have any sentimental attachment to my virginity, I don't want it taken by an act of retaliation against Lucy and Nathan. I'm not holding out for love, but I should probably aim for higher than spite.

After all, there are plenty of reasons besides revenge for wanting a boyfriend. Love, sex, a guaranteed person to hang out with, et cetera. And by the time you're sixteen—if you like boys—having a boyfriend is something you might as well try out.

And I'm a musician! Musicians are not supposed to be virgins who throw up the first and only time they drink beer from a keg. Musicians are not supposed to keep a secret diary in their dresser that dates back to the fourth grade and includes a list of perfect names for kittens. (Top contenders: Captain Fluffington, Mittens, and Meowser.) And speaking of, while musicians *are* supposed to rail against their parental dictators, their main fights are not supposed to revolve around getting said kitten.

Also, a lot of guys are pretty great. Not just Nathan and Ted, but *guys*. Guys are around, abound, aplenty. I've yet to connect with one in any significant way. But they are there.

So I'd already been thinking about them—guys—hypothetically, in general, and thinking about Ted—*the* guy—specifically. Ted is so many things a guy should be. He has great hair. It's light brown and just long enough that it gets wavy near his ears and collar, and it looks soft, like in a fancy conditioner commercial. He's in extracurriculars, which means he cares about the world or at least his college applications. Midway through sophomore year he still looked like a boy in a sea of almost-men, but then he got a little taller and a little filled out. I noticed, but then, suddenly, I Noticed.

And while I'm great at what seems like *enough* things—drums, making smoothies, flying kites (not that I'd done that in a while)—I'm unskilled in the ways of boys, plural, and definitely in the ways of boy, singular.

Reid is, undeniably, a guy, and he's around. I realized if I were to need advice about guys, there was one right in my midst. So, on the first day of school this year, I decided to ask Reid what guys were looking for in a girl. Instead of just answering, he handed me one of his beaten-up notebooks, the ones that he carried with him *everywhere*. Turns out that Reid wasn't just writing lyrics for the Gold Diggers. He was also writing about girls.

Right then, over lunch, we made a pact: We'd help each other figure out the opposite sex and write about it in the notebook. Reid says that "writing keeps us honest," whatever that means.

Neither of us wanted to turn into Lucy or Nathan, even if maybe the unspoken truth was that we were jealous of them and what they had. Nathan was the hot guy in the band, and I guess for some reason I thought maybe I'd be the one to eventually land him. It was probably the same reason that Reid thought the hot girl of the group might be his one day. (The lyrics in "Sugar," one of our earlier songs, about indigo eyes and dreams of demise couldn't be about anyone but blue-eyed, cults-obsessed Lucy, come on.)

Still, jealousy wasn't going to make us liars. And that was something we promised to each other.

*   *   *

Mom's grading papers at our dining room table when I get home. She teaches gender studies at USC, which means she'd be disappointed if she knew I had a notebook with detailed outlines of how to make boys fall in love with me and ways to make Reid appealing to girls. Romance plans in general are probably looked down upon by college professors, so I'm not about to tell Dad, either, even though he's just a professor of American history.

"Riley," she greets me. "You're late."

"Reid wanted to meet me," I say, instead of *THERE WAS A*

HORRIBLE INCIDENT WITH TED CALLAHAN, BUT ALSO HE WAS IN MY CAR. "He needed help with our English lit homework."

"Really?" Her eyebrows knit together. *Worry* is Mom's default emotion for me. Probably when she was my age she was already dissecting the world for gender analysis, not playing in a band and trying to do just enough work in school to get by. "It wasn't about the Gold Diggers?"

"Definitely not." I get a root beer out of the refrigerator and swing the door shut with my foot. "Can I skip dinner? I just ate a waffle."

"A waffle? For dinner?"

"No, not *for* dinner; it's just, now I'm not hungry for dinner." I make an expression I hope makes me seem like a silly kid who doesn't understand how eating and getting full works. "I just want to do my homework and practice for a while."

Her eyes are back on the stack of papers in front of her. "Okay."

"You should do that on your computer," I tell her for the billionth time.

"Eye strain," we say together, and Mom gives me a little smile before I head up to my room.

I speed through my homework and head out to the guesthouse. It sounds swank, but it's hardly bigger than our garage. Mom and Dad had just used it for storage before I'd gotten my first drums, and it took only a week of me playing inside the house for them to consolidate the boxes and crates and move me out here.

I never took offense; I was crappy for a while, and even good drumming is loud and distracting. Plus, having my own space was freeing. Since I wasn't worried about anyone hearing me, I could try anything and everything, and while a lot of it sucked, a lot of it was me getting better.

I was obnoxious about it at first. I wore T-shirts with the Zildjian logo or cutesy illustrations of drum kits. I took my sticks with me everywhere, and when I couldn't get them out, in lieu I'd use two pens on my desktops before, after, and—sometimes—during classes. It was dumb that I was so desperate for everyone to know I was a drummer, but honestly? The only reason I stopped literally wearing it around like an identity was that people finally knew.

My phone buzzes on the floor as I'm practicing rolls. I pick it up and see that it's Lucy. I haven't figured out how to talk to her normally since the Incident. Lucy and I had been on the same page in life since we met. Now I'm trudging along at the same speed, while Lucy is for all intents and purposes an adult.

Before I can even put my phone back it rings again, but this time it isn't someone whose sexual experience intimidates me. It's just Garrick.

"Hi, Riley," he says. "Did you want to review our chemistry notes?"

Poor Garrick is stuck with me for a lab partner. The only experiments I like are the ones where something lights up or changes colors or produces an odor. I thought that was all there was to chemistry, but instead it's usually about measuring liquid into beakers and weighing it before and after you do something that seems inconsequential.

Garrick likes it all. He's going to be a geneticist someday, after he takes a billion more years of school.

"I guess." I work on my double bass technique on my practice pedal, a safe drumming activity to maintain while on the phone. "I think we're okay, though. The test isn't for another week and a half."

"True." He says it like I'm a contestant on a game show, and he's the host congratulating me for getting a question correct. "But I think we should definitely study this weekend."

"I have band practice on Saturday afternoon," I say, "but other than that I'm free." When all I have is band practice, I usually try to fluff up my weekend, make it sound more exciting than it is. Garrick doesn't draw that out of me, though.

"Great, maybe you can come over. My mom will bake cookies." He stops for a moment. "That's lame. I don't know why I said that."

"I like cookies," I say instead of agreeing. Future geneticists are not required to be cool. "So we can review then?"

"Sure. Saturday night?"

When you're in middle school dreaming about being a teenager, you do not expect that instead of going to dances and kissing boys in parked cars, you'll spend your Saturday nights reviewing chem notes.

"Saturday night. Cookies and chemistry."

CHAPTER SEVEN

Top Girls--by Reid

1. <u>Jane Myatt</u>
Jane is firstly really pretty. She has good taste in music (evident by The Le Butcherettes sticker on her car), she dresses cool, and I've been told she has a cat with only three legs she rescued from a shelter, which means she's a good person. Once last year I made a joke about <u>Macbeth</u>, and she said, "That was really funny, Reeve!" It's more important that she thinks that I'm funny than that she gets my name right.

2. <u>Jennie Leung</u>
Jennie is also really pretty, maybe prettier than Jane. Last year she ran a bake sale that benefited The

environment, and she didn't act like it was weird I kept coming back to buy more cookies from her.

3. <u>Erika Ennis</u>

Erika is hot, but in a cool, understated way. Which is less intimidating. She's in the Edendale Spirit Club, which for a lot of people would be pathetic, but it's cool she probably doesn't care what people think. Since she's really smart, I'm hoping she'll be our class valedictorian so our yearbook will document our class as really attractive.

CHAPTER EIGHT

The next morning, I spy Ted alone by his locker. He's methodically organizing his books on a blue plastic shelf that he must have installed himself. I've never used the term *smitten* before, but I am positive I am smitten. If I were a cartoon character, my eyes would be shaped like hearts.

"Hi," I say, and when he doesn't look up, I add, "Ted."

"Hi, Riley." He looks right at me. I did not know eye contact could feel *intimate.*

"Hi," I say again.

"What's up?" He's rummaging through his locker, so I have to watch the back of his head. His hair isn't long, exactly, just a little overgrown. It's like a garden whose owners went out of town for a week. I would like to reach out and touch it, but I don't.

"I, um, the blog?" I bite my lip because no one who isn't a freshman or a transfer student calls it that within the walls of Edendale High School. It was by code name only. "The *Fenching Club. FENCING*, I MEAN!"

What the hell was *FENCHING*! It sounded like *Frenching*. Also I was shouting, and Ted's shoulders shot up like he was under attack. Oh my god.

"Do you want to join?" he asks, as if I hadn't called it by its real name or said *Fenching*.

"I do." Then it's weird in my head because saying *I do* to a cute guy conjures up visions of wedding dresses and floral arrangements. I think of Ted in a tux—hair still ungardened—and he's so cute I smile to myself. Brain Number Two regains control.

"Email me." He emerges from his locker with a stack of textbooks and binders. "Ted at Edendale Fencing Club dot com. I'll send you everything you need." He's off down the hallway.

I've wanted to be a part of the blog since I was a freshman. It's the most countercultural thing our school has to offer, but I've never known how to get involved. Edendale's a private school, but unlike private schools on TV, we don't have to wear goofy uniforms and no one seems freakishly over-achieving. It's obviously been perfectly acceptable for me to be doing only one extracurricular, since the free time I have is supposed to go toward the band. But this is a mission, and I am on it.

"Hey." Lucy bounds up next to me. "Did you get my message last night?"

She still acts like maybe it's bad cell-phone reception. By

now I feel like she'd ask if something was wrong, though she should already know what she did and how small and pointless it made me feel.

"No, sorry." I shrug. Inside my chest, my heart feels caged. Life is basically good: Ashley is annoying, but Mom and Dad are fine, school is also fine, Ted is awkward but maybe attainable (!!!), the band is okay. But without Lucy, *I'm* not fine. Up until this school year started, there wasn't a single day when I didn't risk getting a late slip in one of my classes because it was so much more important to talk to Lucy at her locker instead.

"Did you have Yearbook yesterday?"

I'm pretty sure somewhere Lucy has a list of topics she can still discuss with me. Getting her voice mails, Yearbook, our mutual classes, the band—sort of. The music part of it at least.

"I did. It was mostly boring." If things hadn't changed, I know I'd be dying to tell Lucy every last bit of the car ride with Ted. She'd know everything about Ted! As things stand now, she doesn't even know I like him. And now that she's a lady of experience, I'm too embarrassed to tell her about crushes and nonaction and mermaid books.

"Too bad. Normally, Yearbook's probably a big bucket of excitement," she says.

"You can't carry excitement in a bucket."

"A backpack? A...what do you call those bandanas hobos carry on sticks? A bindle?"

"Excitement *can't* be contained." I nod toward my chemistry classroom. "See you in English lit?"

"Oh, sure," Lucy says with a nod, and I can see how she didn't think our conversation was over yet. She waves before heading off down the hallway. I watch her instead of walking into chemistry, but it's like all I can see is our paths away from each other, dotted lines tracing how separate we've become.

CHAPTER NINE

Top Guys--by Riley

I think this is way too personal of feelings to put in a list! Reid is making me do this.

1. <u>The Crush</u>
   He is smart, handsome, principled, and he has good taste in music. The end!
2. <u>Everyone else</u>
   Not even worth discussing!

CHAPTER TEN

to: ted@edendalefencingclub.com

from: riley.crowe-ellerman@email.com

subject: fencing club!!

hi ted!!

Why am I using so many exclamation points!?! Delete!

to: ted@edendalefencingclub.com

from: riley.crowe-ellerman@email.com

subject: fencing club

dear ted,

how are you today? i'm pretty good. i'm writing to you about fencing club.

Why do I sound like he's my pen pal forced upon me from an interschool correspondence league? Delete!

to: ted@edendalefencingclub.com

from: riley.crowe-ellerman@email.com

subject: fencHing club
just kidding!! what's up for fencing club?

Maybe I shouldn't remind him of how I can barely speak English in his presence and how just maybe that was some kind of Freudian slip brought on by how badly I would like to, among other things, French-kiss him. Wait. Does anyone even call it that? Or was that just in books about teenagers I read when I was twelve?

to: ted@edendalefencingclub.com
from: riley.crowe-ellerman@email.com
subject: anything + everything
you are so smart and so cute and i like your messenger bag and someone told me they saw you at sunset junction last summer so i have a feeling you might have great taste in music and the way i've seen you put on Burt's Bees beeswax lip balm makes me think you're probably a really great kisser so can we just DO THIS, TED, CAN WE?

Yeah, I am not sending that one.

After forty-five minutes, I do not have a masterpiece, but I'm pleased enough to hit send.

to: ted@edendalefencingclub.com
from: riley.crowe-ellerman@email.com

subject: Fencing Club

hi ted,

i'm emailing about the fencing club because i am definitely interested in joining. i don't know if it's like yearbook with staff positions or whatever but i'm not picky, as you probably already know from the roar (like anyone else would have so happily covered the new fertilizer used on the courtyard flowers!).

—riley crowe-ellerman

www.thegolddiggersmusic.com

I tell myself I won't sit at my computer refreshing my inbox, but of course that's what I do. Going downstairs isn't an option. Ashley has friends over, and I'm not up for stepping into their bubble of giggling and eye-shadow experimentation.

My phone seems to radiate its lack of activity, and I remind myself that even if Lucy calls, I won't answer, so what does it matter? I still turn it off and on, just to check, even though I've never done that and had magical missing voice mails or texts appear. But, miraculamazingnessly, when I look back at my computer, there's a (1) beside my inbox.

The bolded, brand-spanking-new email is, indeed, from ted@edendalefencingclub.com.

to: riley.crowe-ellerman@email.com
from: ted@edendalefencingclub.com
subject: RE: Fencing Club

We meet on Thursdays in Ms. Matteson's room right after school. Bring a notepad or a laptop.

Okay, it's not exactly a declaration of love, but it's still amazing Ted Callahan had to think about me and read words I typed. I'm calling it a win for the day.

But then it hits me.

Thursdays are the Gold Diggers' weeknight practice nights. And Thursdays are *important*. It took us forever to come up with a night that didn't conflict with anyone's extra-curriculars or families or Settlers of Catan game nights (okay, that one is just Reid). I'd give up anything for Ted Callahan—like food and water and air—but not my band.

to: ted@edendalefencingclub.com
from: riley.crowe-ellerman@email.com
subject: RE: Fencing Club
this sucks, but I have band practice on thursdays so
I really can't join. thanks for letting me know at least.
if you ever change nights, i'd be totally interested.
—riley
www.thegolddiggersmusic.com

Hopefully that makes me seem responsible and devoted to my craft, qualities I feel like Ted Callahan would appreciate in a person.

Oh man, maybe Reid's right. Maybe Ted *is* a dork.

I'm reading some album reviews at *Pitchfork* and mulling over the Dork Possibility when Ted Callahan makes a glorious return to my inbox.

> to: riley.crowe-ellerman@email.com
> from: ted@edendalefencingclub.com
> subject: RE: Fencing Club
> No problem. It's a good reason to miss it at least!

That's a nice thing to say, and his lightning-fast response makes it almost like we are chatting in real time, which is an awesome fantasy. No, not *awesome*, oh my god. I am not so nerdy that my awesome fantasies should include *INSTANT MESSAGING*.

Then, andIamnotkiddingaboutthis, the (1) is back. Ted, you're back!

> to: riley.crowe-ellerman@email.com
> from: ted@edendalefencingclub.com
> subject: RE: Fencing Club
> Your band's demo tracks are really good. Do you guys have any shows coming up?

I call Reid immediately.

"Yo," he says.

"I think you have to give up 'yo.' I don't think it suits you."

"It *will* suit me," he says. "I'm working on it. What's up?"

"The Crush just sent me a nice email."

"I know it's Ted Callahan. You can just *say* 'Ted Callahan.'"

"TED CALLAHAN JUST SENT ME A NICE EMAIL!"

"What does it say?"

I read it to him. I hate how it doesn't take me any time because that shows it is not exactly a message of epic length.

"It's good, Ri," Reid says. "It's a good sign."

"You're sure?"

"I'm not saying he's taking you to prom. I'm saying it's a good sign." He pauses. "Though 'Walk Around' *is* solid. And I know you don't actually want to go to prom."

"I wish we had a gig coming up," I say. "Not just because of the Crush—"

"Say his name; it's weird now."

"NOT JUST BECAUSE OF TED CALLAHAN. We need a gig. Things have been so weird. We need to feel like a band again."

"We should talk to Nathan," Reid says. "He always seems to know stuff."

"If he knew stuff, wouldn't we already have a gig?"

Reid's silent for a moment, and then another. "Do you ever think about the band breaking up?"

"All the time," I say.

"We'll start something else," he says with confidence, like it's on credit from some cool guy Reid most definitely is not.

"Okay," I say, not because I believe him, but because I want to.

CHAPTER ELEVEN

Qualities About You That Girls Might Like, by Riley

1. Great taste in music (and a good vinyl collection for girls who care about that*)
2. Have your own car and also access to your mom's
3. Know about fancy restaurants**
4. Dress pretty well now
5. Good at enough of school to be smart, not at so much you're a geek
6. Duh, you're in a band!!

*No girls care about that.
**It's thanks to your mom, but you don't have to explain that.

Qualities About You That Guys Might Like, by Reid

1. Really good taste in music
2. Hair is good color and length and Thickness
3. Have fun when you're out, never just stand around looking over it
4. Pretty good body (refuse to go into details, so don't ask)
5. Not popular but everyone seems to like you or think you're cool
6. In a band (duh indeed)

CHAPTER TWELVE

"We should think about scheduling a gig," Reid says at practice the next day.

Nathan and Lucy are leaning over their guitars, tuning up, but they look right up at him.

"What?" Lucy asks. "I couldn't hear you."

"*WE SHOULD SCHEDULE A GIG,*" I say, which is restrained considering the fate of the world, or at least me and Ted, rests on this.

"Are you okay, Riley?" Lucy laughs and goes back to tuning. "Did you have caffeine today?"

"No more than usual," I say. "No, it's just, it's important, getting shows, having people see us."

"Yeah," Reid says, looking right at me, "people, in general."

"Yeah," I say in my Reid voice. Captain Chipmunk. "Not three specific girls or anything."

"What are you guys even talking about?" Nathan strums his guitar a little. The tuning is not good. "Crap, not there."

"Almost," Lucy says like he needs validation.

"What about this?" he says, and they do the thing where they make eye contact and play notes and chords at the same time to make sure they're literally in tune with each other. They've done this forever, way before the Incident, but now I feel like I should leave the room while it happens.

"Riley and I were just saying we should look for gigs." Reid always sounds diplomatic at practice.

"Yeah," Nathan says. "I can talk to my cousin again."

"Why?" I ask. "Is he marrying a second person?"

"Ooh, it's like fundamentalist cults," says Lucy, since she loves reading about cults and other creepy groups of people. "We can learn haunting religious music."

"Reid can grow an old-fashioned beard," I say, which causes Reid to clutch his hands over his bare chin, which probably isn't up for growing a beard, old-fashioned or otherwise, yet. "We can braid our hair."

"Guys." Nathan only needs one word to express how annoying our tangents are. "Jack liked our set, and so maybe he knows someone."

"Great idea," Lucy says.

"I had an idea, too," Reid says.

That's news to me.

"I just thought of this. What about the fall formal?"

"What *about* the fall formal?" Lucy wrinkles her nose. I feel this surge of relief my friend hasn't become obsessed with dances and froufrou dresses and romantic nights in a school gym just because she has a boyfriend.

"They sometimes hire a band, right? Why not us?"

Actually, it isn't a bad idea. All of us agree.

"It's in a few weeks," Nathan says. "We have to move fast on this."

"I'll talk to Ms. Belman tomorrow," Reid says. For his free period he's an office assistant. "I don't know where they normally find bands for events."

"It doesn't count as *going* to the fall formal if you just play there, does it?" I ask. I'm not against high school functions in general, but even with my Hunt for Ted Callahan in full swing, the thought of intentionally going to a school dance makes me feel like the kind of person I never want to be.

"Definitely not, Ri," Reid says. "We can still be cool."

We all laugh at that and start playing our newest song, "Garage." It's sloppy, but it's starting to sound like an actual song and not all of us just randomly jamming. The moment when that happens is like magic, how it all gels together and settles into something bigger than the four of us and our instruments.

I remember always loving music. Dad played CDs constantly when I was little, and I thought all kids grew up listening to Nirvana and the Pixies nonstop. When I was in kindergarten and everyone else thought they'd grow up to be firemen or nurses or horses (to be fair, that was just Holly Long, and she's still weird), I insisted I'd grow up to be a rock star. (I accompanied these declarations with drawings of me looking like David Bowie.) By now everyone else wants to be lawyers and professional bloggers and geneticists, but I'm still on the path to being a rock star. If I didn't believe that, I couldn't see the point.

After practice I rush out after Reid (and it's hard to rush with your drums in tow) because I figure Nathan and Lucy want alone time. Today Nathan's right behind us, though, and then Lucy appears.

"Can you hang out?" she asks, and I realize she's talking to me. "Mom got all of these berries at the farmers' market today, and I was going to make fancy lemonades."

"Oh, um." I look at Reid like he's going to save me. Those words echo in my head—*save me*—and I wonder if I'm stupid for needing to be saved from the girl who was my best friend. *Is* my best friend? Plus, fancy lemonades sound great! "Reid and I were going to work on a thing."

"Yes," Reid says quickly. "Lots of work to do."

Saving me. Actually. The way best friends do. It's weird how that switched around.

"Do you need help?" she asks. "I don't have to make the lemonades tonight."

"No," I say as quickly as a person can. "No thank you, I mean."

She watches us for a couple moments. I've stood by Lucy so many times when she was worried about something, so I know this is exactly how she looks. Back when the something wasn't me, I would have done anything to take the blank look from her eyes, to make her nearly constant smile reappear.

But the something *is* me.

"Okay, Riley. See you tomorrow."

I wave and finish loading my car. Reid hangs nearby and watches me. It's good we don't have to say much to know what's going on with the other.

"Can you really talk to Ms. Belman tomorrow?" I ask.

"Yeah, it's no big deal," he says. "I should have thought of it before."

"You should have." But I smile because I'm kidding. Mostly.

"I have to go do a thing," he says. "I didn't have time to tell you earlier, but it's all in here."

I catch the Passenger Manifest as he tosses it to me. It's impressive because if you combined our athletic abilities, you might come up with the skills of a sad kindergartner. "Go do a thing. We have Family Night tonight."

"Rock on with that."

CHAPTER THIRTEEN

<u>The Sad Animal Project, by Reid</u>

I learned today that Jane works as a
volunteer at Paws for People, which is this
animal rescue charity that finds homes
for abandoned animals. She couldn't be a
better person.

So I'm going to "accidentally" walk past
Paws for People tonight. Next door there's an
organic coffee place that's pretty cool, so
I'll go there and then "stumble across" the
rescue place. Jane will be there, and I can
pretend to really consider getting some sad
animal.

Then tomorrow I can talk to her some
more about it, show her how I'm researching
whatever its health condition is or maybe
what breed it is, and do this for a while so

we have to talk every day. Then finally I
will have to tell her I literally just found out
my brother's allergic, so I can't. But by then
she'll be used to talking to me every day,
so we'll keep doing that and before long
maybe she'll fall in love with me. And since
I'm already in love with her, it'll be great
and easy once it actually starts.

Probably she'll be volunteering with
some jerky douchebag and none of this will
actually happen, though. I won't even go in
if I spot any jerky douchebags.

Crap. This is doomed.

CHAPTER FOURTEEN

I don't know if Family Nights were Mom's or Dad's idea, because they present everything as a United Front. The two of them read more books than people in, like, library school, so I'm sure it was advice from some parenting manual that led them down this road. Tonight at least we're out at the Palace, which isn't as fancy as its name would have you believe but is pretty much my favorite Chinese food around.

"What's new with you, Riley?" Mom asks. "Besides the Gold Diggers?"

Apparently, I had been communicating by always answering every question about what was going on by mentioning the band and only the band. I can't help that it's the most important thing in my life, and, anyway, do Mom and Dad really want to hear about Lucy and Nathan doing it or how wonderfully worn-in Ted's hoodie looks?

"Yearbook's okay," I say.

"*The Roar!*" Dad says with a crazy grin. It's a pretty lame name for a yearbook, but Dad thinks it's the Weirdest Ever. "I wish—"

"That every school's yearbook was the sound their mascot made?" It's not a bad joke, but he's only made it twenty-seven thousand times.

Ashley rolls her eyes with flair she probably picked up from reality TV villains who aren't there to make friends. For once I am totally on her side.

"Anything else?" Mom asks, as if Dad hasn't interrupted and I haven't interrupted him. I think this is how Mom maintains her sanity.

"Not really," I say.

Mom and Dad share a look like they're forming a mind meld to decide whether or not I'm joining a cult or doing drugs or being the worst student Edendale High School's ever seen.

"Aren't you going to ask what's up with me?" Ashley asks.

"Absolutely, Ashley," Mom says, folding her hands in her lap and looking right at Ashley. "What's new with you?"

Ashley tells a long and confusing story about her friends Jenica and Hayley and their usual lunch table, and I'm sure the insides of my parents' brains are flashing images of the smart and articulate and yet easily-amused-by-the-same-joke-ten-times children they expected to produce.

Lucy calls while I'm out, and since it's been crazy long since we've talked on the phone, and because I feel bad about my lack of involvement with the fancy lemonades, I call her back when we get home. She answers with an enthusiasm that makes me feel like a bad person. I wonder if I am a bad person. I wonder if she is, too, in a different way from my bad-person-ness. I wonder if everyone is a bad person, somewhere, deep down. Probably not Jane Myatt, with her constant attention to the rescue of damaged, overstocked, and irregular animals. Probably not Garrick, with his devotion to school and science and the quest to end diseases that get you just because of who you're born as. And probably not Ted Callahan, because I've spent a lot of time wondering what's inside his head and heart, and there's never been one hypothetical bad item of note.

"My parents can be so annoying," I say. It is the safest topic ever. "Ugh, have you started your English lit yet?"

"Yeah, I worked on it for a while. It isn't bad once you get going."

Lucy always says things like this, but it's only because she's smarter than I am.

"Do you think we could really end up playing the dance?" she asks. "Sometimes I feel like Nathan and Reid have these ideas that are more than we can actually do."

I start to agree with her, but my brain gets stuck on the idea of divulging secret inner-band opinions to her of all people and—sweet merciful gods of timing, Reid is calling.

"I have to go," I say. "Sorry. Mom needs my help downstairs."

"See you tomorrow," she says. "Are you doing anything after school?"

"I don't know, I'll check," I say as if I actually will. "Bye."

I click over. "Hey. How did the Sad Animal Project go?"

"Oh man, Riley." He is smiling so wide I can hear it. "I'm so in."

CHAPTER FIFTEEN

<u>The Sad Animal Project, Continued, by Reid</u>

Last night may have been the best night of my life.

I'll back up. When I walked by Paws for People, I didn't see Jane at all. There was a guy working, but he wasn't a douchebag—he was like a dad type. So I started to go in. But then I thought, wait, maybe that guy actually is Jane's dad. So here are the problems with that:

1. If Jane and I end up going out, I want to plan out what to say and what I'm wearing when I meet her parents. It can't just be some random day when I have on a random T-shirt and when I have nothing composed to say to them.

2. I actually always get along really well with *people's parents*. One of the worst things that ever happened to my rep was when I went to Darcy Levien's party freshman year and ended up talking to her parents all night about their vinyl. Come on! They had a freaking awesome collection! Original Nirvana! Sub Pop Bleach! They were way more interesting than anyone else there. But on Monday morning, even though stuff went down like Ryan Holland and Michaela Brewster hooking up, and Logan Perry throwing up in Jesse Torres's good-luck hat, all these people were talking about what a loser I was for staying in the house all night and not going out to the backyard where the party was. Writing it out now, I guess I can see how I was kind of a loser. Still--the Slits' "Typical Girl" 7-inch! The Voidoids' Destiny Street--and not the Razor & Tie reissue, the Red Star Records original pressing. Amazing. My point's that if Jane walks out of the back room or wherever else she could be while I'm bonding with her dad, any forgotten memories of me being a loser

and hanging out with parents are going to rush to the surface and she will never fall in love with me.

3. I'm only doing this to talk to Jane in the first place. I'm not wasting time pretending to love disabled pets for any other reason.

So I walk over to Silverlake Coffee and the barista's pretty cute so I try to talk to her but she seems busy and I don't want to be disrespectful to Jane so after I kill some time I walk back and she's there.

I go in and she smiles and says, "Hi, Reid," which is awesome. She knows my name! We talk about world history, and how Mr. Agos's tests don't seem fair but we do okay on them so we're not too worried. She asks me about the Gold Diggers, and I tell her how we might play at the fall formal, and she tells me to let her know for sure because she's not usually into dances but she'd go if we were playing. Which is amazing. I tell her I'll let her know, and I give her a Gold Diggers button, which she pins to her jacket. Without hesitation!

The dad-type guy comes out of the back and says Jane has to walk some of the dogs, and I think he's waiting to get me alone so he can yell at me, but I guess Jane did have to walk dogs because this guy just takes over answering questions about dogs, and he decides I would get along really well with this dog with only one eye for some reason. All the dogs there have something wrong with them so there's probably no symbolism in that.

I hang out with the dog for a while so that Jane comes back in before I go, and I act like I'm going to go home and talk to my mom and I make a big deal out of how much I love this dog and so Jane seems happy and actually so does the dad-type guy and Jane is still wearing the button (not like I thought she'd take it off outside but I did think it was a possibility) so I say good-bye because it feels like I'm leaving on a high note.

Jane says to hang on, and she puts all the dogs back where they're supposed to go, and she walks out with me and hugs me! She says it's great I care about animals, and she's crossing her fingers everything works out for me and this dog. So I thank her and act like I feel the same way about the dog and leave.

It was an amazing evening.

CHAPTER SIXTEEN

Saturday night I stop at Albertsons on my way to Garrick's to buy some root beer and Nerds because I feel like being a good guest. Garrick's house is up in the hills past the Shakespeare Bridge, which is not that fancy or big a bridge to be the namesake of the most famous writer of all time. It's like naming our guesthouse the Beatles Manor.

"Hi, Riley." Garrick opens the front door of the sage-and-white house tucked behind a ridiculous number of palm trees. You have no idea whose parents think stuff like extra palm trees are important when you're at school together, but the second you walk up to someone's house for the first time, all these details come spilling forth.

"I brought Nerds," I tell him. "And root beer."

"Cool. I love root beer," he says with a big smile. "Come on in."

"Thanks for inviting me over," I say. "This is way better than the library. I don't trust any place with a Leonardo DiCaprio computer wing."

"He did donate a lot of money for those computers,"

Garrick says. "But this will be better. My parents are out, so we should be able to get a lot of studying done."

"Rock on," I say, walking inside and glancing around the front room, which is the kind of eclectic that doesn't happen naturally. Mismatched artwork and photographs and posters decorate the walls, a purple throw rug covers most of the hardwood floor, and none of the furniture matches. Garrick's dad is a TV director, so I assume the chaos is strictly on purpose. Fancy creative people love chaos. It's weird someone could love chaos and also breed to produce Garrick, geneticist in training, but probably no more so than my academic parents ending up with me.

Garrick and I settle in the living room with our books, him on the couch and me on the floor. I am way more interested in the as-promised fresh chocolate chip cookies Garrick's mom left for us than studying, but I manage both.

"What is the name of NaClO?" he asks me.

"Mffffwww," I say, because my mouth is stuffed full of hot, melty, salty-sweet chocolate chip action. I wonder why more songs aren't written, monuments aren't built, wars aren't fought over chocolate chip cookies.

"Wrong," he says. "It's sodium hypochlorite."

"It's really weird you knew what I said," I say, and he laughs.

"I know. But I did. Okay, diamond is composed of what bonds?"

Of course I'd already reached for another cookie, so: "Mmmvvnt?"

"Perfect, yeah, covalent."

I pump my fist like I just scored a home run or some other sports thing. "These are basically the best cookies I've ever had."

"They're pretty great," he says. "Oh, you probably want to turn music on, right? I can turn some music on."

"Yeah, I study way better with music," I say, even though I'm scared about the kind of tunes a future geneticist rocks out to. So I toss him my iPod, and he hooks it up to the stereo and plays an Allo Darlin' album, and maybe it's just because it's one of the first alphabetically, but, still, good selection.

"Your turn," he says. "Quiz me."

I swipe his flash cards even though this seems pointless. Garrick knows everything there is to know about science, and he proves that point right by... well, knowing everything I ask him. It's so predictable that when I ask "If you have two-point-five moles of oxygen, you need how many moles of hydrogen for complete combustion?" and he answers "Five" and I tell him "Nope! Try again, contestant!" it's clear I'm just being stupid and of course he's right.

"You're going to do fine," I tell him.

"You'll do good, too," he says, less enthusiastically, but I think he means it. "So, are you going to the fall formal?"

"Reid's trying to see if we can play at the dance," I say. "Are you?"

"I was seeing if you wanted to go," he says.

Oh, oh, oh, WHAT!

"No!" I say. I kind of shout it, actually. I sound like a Grade A jerk. "I just mean—I can't. I'll either play or I won't go. I don't like school functions."

"Except Yearbook."

"Except Yearbook, yeah. That's just because I know I have to have some extracurriculars to get into a decent college." I shrug because I would rather dwell on Yearbook and college than this weird possibility that *DID GARRICK JUST ASK ME OUT?*

I look over at him and try to evaluate him as a new person, as if I didn't know he liked DNA and molecules and got excited about his mom's cookies. Okay, to be fair, I was pretty excited about his mom's cookies, too. And Garrick is no Ted Callahan (who is?), but he isn't reprehensible. His dark blond hair is shaggy in front, which I approve of, and he's wearing jeans and a T-shirt, which is boring but isn't a sin, either. (To be fair, most of the time Ted Callahan wears jeans and T-shirts, too, though his are always faded in this perfect vintage manner.) Garrick's body is kind of shaped like that of a Lego man—rectangular torso and stick legs—but that's nothing awful.

Wait, what is going on? Why am I evaluating Garrick like a dude and not a lab partner, and did he actually just ask me out?

"Extracurriculars are a smart idea," he says.

The subject seems firmly changed, and I am firmly okay with that. The flash cards come back out, but I am now juggling thoughts about the potential ask-out, about shaggy hair, about being alone on a Saturday night with a boy who isn't Reid.

Which is how I end up joining Garrick on the couch. I make a face like it's weird that I'm there, and he laughs, and I touch his hair, *SINCE IT'S NOT LIKE I'VE GOTTEN TO TOUCH TED'S*, and I guess it is very much a foregone conclusion we are going to kiss, but what I am not expecting at all is that Garrick is actually a crazy good kisser. Perfect amount of pressure, moisture, lips he clearly uses balm on, good breath, good use of tongue. Check, check, check, perfect kissing report card, Garrick.

What is happening?!

"I'm going to have some Nerds." I reach for candy while I regret my choice of words because I am *TOTALLY HAVING A NERD, AREN'T I*. Wait, is Garrick even a nerd? Is it that he just likes science and doesn't seem to have much of a social life? I am a freaking rock star and I was free on a Saturday, too. Seriously, the world is upside-down and outside-in.

The Passenger Manifest is in my purse, practically beckoning me to detail what is going on. If it had the technology, it would be sending out its version of the Bat Signal to Reid.

"I'll have some, too," he says, holding his hand out. Garrick isn't acting awkward at all. Garrick is a master of making out: he's good at it and he doesn't act like it altered the course of time and space afterward.

"Should we study more?" I ask. It's the first time in the

history of Garrick and Riley, Chemistry Lab Partners, that I am the one to suggest more studying.

"Yes." He smiles and grabs for the flash cards again. As if studying makes him so happy. Okay, I know studying does make him happy. He's the master of making out and studying.

Studying: expected. Making out: the opposite.

"If a reaction releases heat, it is a *what* kind of reaction?" he asks.

"Exothermic?" I guess. I'm right!

"Your turn." He passes the cards to me.

Our hands touch for a second, and it isn't electric, and it isn't exciting, but our hands are touching, and not long ago our freaking lips and faces were touching, and I may have touched the heck out of his shaggy hair, and *IS IT NORMAL WE AREN'T SAYING ANYTHING ABOUT THAT?*

No, seriously, I have no idea. Is it?

CHAPTER SEVENTEEN

Romance Playlist, by Reid

1. The Luckiest Guy on the Lower East Side--Magnetic Fields
2. Speedy Marie--Frank Black
3. The Luckiest--Ben Folds
4. The Blues Are Still Blue--Belle & Sebastian
5. Talk about the Passion--R.E.M.
6. Punk Rock Girl--The Dead Milkmen
7. I Want To Be The Boy To Warm Your Mother's Heart--The White Stripes
8. Such Great Heights--The Postal Service
9. All I Need--Radiohead
10. Lola--The Kinks
11. You Said Something--PJ Harvey
12. Jesus, Etc.--Wilco
13. Do You Realize??--The Flaming Lips

14. When My Baby's Beside Me--Big Star
15. Go Places--The New Pornographers

Songs for Love and Sex, by Riley

1. Modern Love--David Bowie
2. You're So Great--Blur
3. Step into My Office, Baby--Belle & Sebastian
4. Strange Currencies--R.E.M.
5. Always Looking--Dum Dum Girls
6. Maps--Yeah Yeah Yeahs
7. Damn Girl--Justin Timberlake featuring will.i.am
8. Friday I'm in Love--The Cure
9. Anyone Else but You--The Moldy Peaches
10. Take Me with U--Prince
11. Yeah You--Andrew Mothereffing Jackson
12. By Your Side--Beachwood Sparks
13. Take Me Anywhere--Tegan and Sara
14. Whole Wide World 4 England--Wreckless Eric
15. When You're Young--The Jam
16. Free Money--Patti Smith

CHAPTER EIGHTEEN

"We need to talk." Approximately fourteen hours have passed since the Garrick Incident, so I'm positive I say it calmly into the phone.

"We do," Reid replies. "Meet at Fred Sixty-Two?"

"Now?" I ask.

"Yeah. Now."

I leave my room and barely fully enunciate a "meeting Reid" to Mom and Dad, who are huddled over Dad's iPad trying to solve a crossword puzzle together. It takes no time to get to Fred 62, but parking is horrible, and I see Reid strutting like an old-timey dude while I'm circling and praying to whatever's out there that a space opens up.

"Did you see?" Reid greets me when I finally walk up. "My car is right around the corner. Parking magic."

"Yeah, yeah," I say.

"A lot to talk about," he says. "Let me see the book."

My stomach is grumbling for a waffle, so I'm hoping we

can get food into our systems before conversation or note-booking really begins. "In a minute."

"Riley," he says, then "Riley" again, the way you talk to a dog that isn't listening to your commands.

"Fine." I whip out the Passenger Manifest from my bag and smack him against the chest with it. "Take it back. There's a lot I need to add but—"

"Good."

"Good? How do you know? Oh my god," I say. *"ARE YOU FRIENDS WITH GARRICK?"*

He looks confused. "Garrick Bell?"

I just nod.

"No—I mean, I know him, we have a bunch of classes together, we've hung out before but—" He appraises me with a look. "Why?"

We walk inside and sit down at a booth in the back.

"So what happened with Garrick Bell?" Reid asks.

"We were just hanging out studying," I say.

"On a Saturday night?" Reid asks.

"It's when we were both free," I say. "So it was normal, and then I think he asked me to the fall formal—"

"You *think*?"

"Trust me, it was vague."

"What did he say?"

"He asked if I was going, and when I said we might be playing, he said he was seeing if I wanted to go."

"Riley." Reid shakes his head like a wise old sage on top of a mountain. "He was clearly asking you."

"No. *Clearly* would be, 'Hey, Riley, do you want to go to the dance with me as my date?' This was totally not *clearly*."

"So what did you say?"

"Just that I'd only be going if we played." I shrug. "You don't have to hear all this stuff if you don't want to."

When we started divulging all of this stuff to each other, I never thought I would end up making out with frigging Garrick Bell, after all. *MUCH LESS LIKING IT.*

"No, tell me," Reid says.

"Well...thenwesortofmessedaround," I say, even though I've never said *messed around* before in my life, and if all you do is kiss with your front halves kind of smushed together and maybe an "accidental" boob touch or four, does that count as messing around?

"Whoa," Reid says.

"And here's the superweird thing," I say as if nothing I've said yet has been superweird. "Garrick is a really good kisser."

"No, I can see that."

I almost miss the table as I set down my glass of water. *"WHAT?"*

Reid nearly knocks his own water over. "I didn't mean it like that!"

I swat my menu at his head. "Why are you analyzing Garrick Bell's kissing skills?"

"Ow, Riley, stop it." He unsuccessfully blocks my every blow. "No, just because of Sydney."

"Sydney who?"

"You don't know?" Reid laughs, stops, then gets swept away by more laughter.

"I DON'T KNOW. TELL ME."

"Sydney Jacobs," he says, "went out with Garrick last year. Before he transferred to Edendale. I thought people knew that."

It's not that Sydney Jacobs is *that* famous. Okay, actually, yes, she's famous, maybe more than a little, especially if you are under twelve, which until this year Ashley was. So I am well aware that Sydney Jacobs plays the lazy but aggressive best friend on *eJenni*, which I'm pretty sure never stops playing on Nickelodeon. So, no, she is not a rock star and she's not even a movie star, but she's *something*, and Garrick has dated that *something*. Probably messed around with that *something*.

Ohmygodwhatifhetotallydidit with that *something*.

"It's weird you didn't know that," Reid says, like he's an expert on everything.

"Crap," I manage to say.

"Yeahhhh," Reid says.

"So what about you?" I ask Reid. I'm sick of imagining how adorable and spunky Sydney must have looked all the time. I messed around with Garrick while wearing faded jeans and an even more faded Sleater-Kinney T-shirt. Not that clothes matter, but Garrick clearly could do and has done a lot better than me.

Reid smirks. "I'm glad you asked."

CHAPTER NINETEEN

<u>The Sad Animal Project, Continued, by Reid</u>

When I got in my car after practice I had a voice mail. It was Jane, seeing if I'd talked to my mom about the dog yet. I called Paws for People right away, and she answered, and just like last time we start talking right away, but this time she can't talk for long since she's on the work phone and she can't tie it up.

I just decide to do it, so I ask if I should just stop by so I can finish our conversation and see the dog.

She says yes.

Luckily this time the dad-type guy isn't working, since I guess Saturday nights are pretty slow. So it's just us, and we talk about everything, her family, my family, dogs, music, school, seriously, anything you can imagine we probably talked about it. She has to walk all the dogs before the overnight guy shows up, so I help out, and once she's off I suggest we get coffee at the Brite Spot and she says yes to that, too.

We drive separately which is kinda disappointing but once we get there we're back to talking nonstop. She is seriously amazing, so the whole time I'm working up how I'm going to kiss her once we leave, but I can't because we have to sort of naturally split up to get to our cars. Next time I will figure out how to kiss her.

CHAPTER TWENTY

When I get home on Sunday afternoon, I ignore Mom and Dad, who are making a big production out of making homemade salsa in the kitchen, and head straight for my room. Googling "Sydney Jacobs" doesn't make her less adorable or well dressed or famous. I try "Sydney Jacobs + Garrick Bell" and results spew out like molten lava from a volcano.

It turns out I am far from the first to notice Garrick's shaggy hair because tween girls have been raving about it, on top of his "kissable lips" (well...!), "sweet smile" (not inaccurate), and "awesome sense of style" (not taking your side on that one, tweens, not like I'm one to talk) ever since Garrick was Sydney's date to the Kids' Choice Awards earlier this year. There are *MULTIPLE IMAGES* of the two of them on the silly orange-not-red carpet being all coupley and happy.

In lieu of documenting this, I print out three of the pictures to paste into the Passenger Manifest once I get it back from Reid. Then I go downstairs and turn on the TV to see if I can catch Sydney in action. Of course *eJenni* is on. The studio audience or laugh track goes nuts for her, and she looks great in an awesome jacket and nicer jeans than the United Front think jeans need to be. I feel like a goober in comparison.

Ashley walks into the room and stares at the TV screen. "Why are you watching this?"

I try to think of a reasonable explanation that does not involve any Garrick-kissing. I change the channel to MSNBC and shrug.

"Just worrying about our crumbling American society."

Ashley makes a face. "There's an *America's Next Top Model* marathon on. Can I watch that instead?"

With a heavy sigh I agree, but then I stick around to at least watch the makeovers. Watching beautiful people cry about their hair is way preferable to thinking about Sydney Jacobs any longer.

* * *

At school the next morning I wait for the crowds to part and for me to be revealed as a Garrick-kissing, Nerds-having, science-learning fool who thinks she's entitled to the kind of boys celebrities sleep with. But it's just Monday.

"Hey, Riley," Ted says as I head from my locker to chemistry. My cartoon heart does a cartwheel.

"Hi." I try to sound calm.

"Sorry you can't join *Fencing Club*."

"Me too!" I sort of shout.

"Okay," he says. "See you."

"Oh, I—I meant to email you back." I had, but I'd hoped a magical gig would appear immediately. "But thanks for what you said about the band."

"Well," he says, with a shrug, "you guys are really good. Hopefully, I can come see you play sometime."

"I'll let you know, yeah." I realize I am *FULL-OUT GRINNING* at him.

I wait for him to wave and walk off, but he doesn't. We're still standing together.

"When did you start playing drums?"

"About three years ago."

"Cool," he says, then smiles.

It hits me that even though this is barely a conversation, it's nice. Ted is not just good hair and impressive extracurriculars. Ted is a guy I can just stand and talk to, and it's normal. Ted, it's normal!

"Hey." Lucy walks up. Maybe if Edendale were a bigger school, I could avoid her a little more. Lucy notices I'm talking to Ted, and kind of steps back so she isn't being rude. I suddenly want to cry that I can't give her a secret look to indicate maybe Something Is Happening. I miss Lucy so freaking much.

"See you in world history." Ted walks off.

Then *Lucy* gives *me* a Look! "Are you friends with him?"

"I guess." I try to affect a casual pose, which is weird when you're standing in the middle of the hallway because I associate casualness with leaning, and there is no leaning to be had. "Why?"

"He's cute in a weird way, isn't he?"

"Yes," I say very automatically. "I mean, I guess. I mean, what's weird, really?"

Lucy laughs. "Good point."

"I, uh, should go." I walk into the bathroom, but I don't even have to go. I just wash my hands and walk back out. By then, Lucy's out of sight.

Garrick's walking down the hallway, and I give him a wave I decide is appropriate after the messing around as well as the Sydney Jacobs discovery.

He hands me my hoodie. "You left your jacket thing at my house."

Wait, Garrick doesn't know the word for hoodie? What kind of genius are you, Garrick?

"Thanks." I wonder if anyone walking by knows what happened based on this hoodie exchange. I still would have forgotten it there if we hadn't messed around, wouldn't I?

No, I totally would not have.

Besides the various weirdnesses of the morning, the day is typical. But after school I have a plan of making a random thing a regular thing.

"Riley!" Reid comes tearing around the corner toward my locker, breathing exactly the way a guy who never runs would with all this tearing around. "Good news!"

"Jane?" I ask.

"We, my friend," he says with the grace and dignity of an old-fashioned movie star, "are playing the fall formal."

"YES!" I high-five him, and even think about hugging him, but hugging makes people talk and probably enough people think since Lucy and Nathan were secretly Doing It that Reid and I are, too. "You're awesome for making this happen."

Reid grins like he is aware of his own awesomeness. I let it slide.

"I'm gonna go find Luce and Nathan. Come with me."

"I have to do a thing, a potential Time With the Crush thing," I say. "So I should go."

"Good luck with that." He smirks and hands me the Passenger Manifest.

"Shut up," I say. "And thanks for the fall formal gig."

"Hey, it's for all of us," he says. "And we did it by having great demos."

I grin at him and head off down the hallway. I don't make it all the way to Ted's locker before he walks up right beside me. It's a sign! Thanks, universe. Love, Riley.

"Hey, Ted." I approach carefully, the way you do with bunny rabbits and motion-detector singing-and-dancing Santas. "I was wondering if you needed a ride."

It's a bold move.

"Really?" he asks.

"Really," I say, but I try to make it all easy breezy.

"Okay, if you don't mind," he says. "And I have to talk to Ms. Matteson for a couple minutes."

"No problem, I can meet you by your locker," I say. "Not that I know where your locker is. I mean, it's alphabetical, I sort of know. Not by heart, not the number, just, in general, it's near Mrs. Bullard's room, I think, right, is it?"

Oh my god, Riley. Shut up.

But Ted just says, "Cool!" and disappears back into Ms. Matteson's classroom.

I try to appear casual and as if I only have the vaguest notion of Ted's locker location, and he's out like he says in just a couple minutes and then we're off down the hallway together.

"Should I take you to your mom's office again?" I ask him.

"Yeah," he says.

I wait for him to expand on that or talk about anything else, but he doesn't. I know Ted's social circle is Toby Singer, Jon Banas, Brendon Maro, and Brendon's girlfriend, Aisha Osman. Even when I catch a glimpse of that table at lunch it's not like Ted's the life of the party. So I'm accepting that maybe he's quiet and it means nothing about my chances with him.

"We have a show coming up." I blurt it out as I'm letting us into the car.

"Oh yeah?" Ted asks me.

"Yeah, at the fall formal" shoots out of my mouth, which is clearly back to depending on Brain Number Two for its information. I now have no need, no pending information for an email later! How am I supposed to lure Ted into my affections without pending information? "Are you going? Do you have a date or something?"

And so now I have no pending information *and* I asked a supernosy question I'm not even sure I want the answer to. If Garrick Bell could have sex with celebrities, what is Ted Callahan capable of? Real rock stars? I have no chance.

"I, uh, yeah, I don't have a date," he says, kind of blushing (!!!). "But I want to see you guys play. So maybe I'll just go."

"You should go," I say really forcefully, like there's a blood shortage and he's the only one left with Type A. "Go! I'll be there! We can hang out."

"Yeah, okay," he says, like I've talked him into it. Humanity will survive on the blood of Ted Callahan! "I'll think about going."

I pull up to his mom's office building, and his door swings open and he's out. Considering I all but just asked him out, it's a swifter exit than I want.

"See you, Riley," he says with a wave. "Thanks for the ride."

"Anytime, Ted!" I call instead of something low-key and cool. I think there is a scary but real chance I am not capable of being low-key and cool. It's bad news for anyone, particularly a rock star.

CHAPTER TWENTY-ONE

Places To Take Someone That Could Be
Romantic, by Reid

1. <u>LAMILL</u>
   Yeah, it's just a coffee shop, but it's fancy and
   expensive, and they're open later than Silverlake
   Coffee. You can walk there from the Satellite,
   so it'd be a good quiet place to take someone
   before a show. Also they have that shot of
   espresso that tastes like a jelly doughnut, and I
   bet you could blow a girl's mind with it.
2. <u>Griffith Observatory</u>
   One of the most romantic things you can do
   with someone is look at the stars together.
3. <u>Edendale Grill</u>
   I haven't been here, but some guy took my
   mom on a date here once and she said it
   was <u>very</u> romantic, which isn't something you
   want your mom to tell you, but I still noted it.

CHAPTER TWENTY-TWO

I don't have much homework, so after I drop off Ted, I drive down Sunset to Amoeba Music, where I have probably logged more hours than any other building except school or home. Reid's a snob about actual vinyl, and Lucy's in love with her iPod, and while I have a record player as well as my own iPod, CDs are easy and go right into my car stereo, and I love picking up these shrink-wrapped square plastic boxes knowing they very well could contain something super life-changing.

Mondays are a weird day to shop for music, since new releases are out on Tuesdays, but at this point I'm mainly catching up on things. I can only afford to buy one CD today thanks to the sad amount of cash Mom and Dad call an allowance. I'd love to get a job, like here or maybe one of the cooler coffee shops on Sunset, but my parents enforced their United Front to let me know my priority should be school, and also that there was nothing I desperately needed that couldn't be paid out of my allowance.

Obviously the parents and I have different definitions of *desperately.*

My phone buzzes in my pocket, and it seems like the right timing to be Lucy, but it's Reid.

"Hey, what are you doing?" he asks. "Can we talk about algebra homework?"

"I'm at Amoeba right now."

"Whoa," he says, as if we're both four years old and I'm next in line to see Santa.

"It's just Amoeba," I say, and it's not all the way out of my mouth before I feel guilty, and stroke a CD bin with my free hand to let the store know I don't think of it as a *just*. "I mean, we go a lot."

"Together," he says. "We go *together*."

"Are you mad I didn't invite you?"

"No," he says. "I'm pointing out, Ri, that this could be *very* good for you. Look around right now."

I do. The store's not packed, but there are plenty of people flipping through CDs. Big deal.

"Most people are alone," he says. "Right?"

Actually that's true.

"You could meet someone there," he says. "Someone cooler than—"

"Shut up," I say, though I guess that both guys I like are maybe not the coolest. "People are alone to buy music. It's serious. That's it."

"That's why *you're* there alone," Reid says. "Just keep an open mind. That's all I'm saying."

"See you." I click the phone off. For a moment I look

around to see if people are hitting on each other like I imagine they do in skeezy bars. It's boring compared to actual CD shopping, so my attention's back on the album quest.

"Hey, can I see that?"

I've just found the reissue of the Sandwiches' *Getting It,* and am not about to hand it over. But when I glance up to see the person the nondescript voice is attached to, it turns out the voice is not an accurate indicator of nondescriptiveness. Cute guy, record shop, CD in common, hello and welcome to the best moment ever, Riley.

Reid might be right.

"It's the last copy," I say, not to play hard to get, but because it's the last copy and this cute boy is not weaseling his way into stealing it from me just because he has eyes the color of dark clouds, spiky, well-coiffed blond hair, one more facial piercing than my parents would deem acceptable (so, one total), and a Coyote Dreams T-shirt.

"I know it's the last copy." He smiles like he's flirting. Maybe he's flirting! Maybe Reid is 100 percent right! "That's why I'm asking to see it."

"You can see it"—I hold it in front of him—"but it's mine."

"That's fair." He reaches out and holds the CD steady by wrapping his hand around my wrist. I suddenly feel like we've gotten to second base or something.

"I like your shirt," I say while he's examining the CD, not because it's particularly a great shirt or anything, but so he'll know that I know Coyote Dreams.

"Thanks." He releases my wrist. I'm, I realize, disappointed. "You for sure getting this?"

"I'm totally for sure getting it. Yup."

Yup? Since when do I say *yup?* I'm suddenly Riley the Cowgirl.

"Well, you did beat me to it," he says, "so it's fair. If you change your mind, though, you can call me, I'll buy it from you."

"What?" I squint at him while he takes a pen out of his jeans pocket and scrawls a phone number onto my hand without even asking permission. "They can probably order you one, even though it's used, or maybe you can check—"

It hits me as I'm talking that this is how guys hit on girls, and not just the best way this guy can think of to procure this album.

"Okay," I say, like that will mind-wipe him of the string of stupidity I just spewed forth. "If I decide to sell it, you're my first call."

"Or even if you're thinking about it," he says with a smile. It's not quite as good a smile as Ted's, but it comes way easier to him. "I'm Milo."

"I'm Riley." I shake his hand, but carefully, so the ink won't smudge. I want to photograph it for evidence for the Passenger Manifest, because this is a big moment.

"Good to meet you, Riley."

I try to gauge how old he is. Maybe a year older than me? A senior?

I realize I haven't spoken for a couple moments, and it's verging on weird. "Good to meet you, too!"

"I have to run," he says.

Where to, Milo? Milo, is there another girl? Milo, are you doing something cool, like getting in line for a secret show no one told me about? Milo, please tell me you're off to your own band practice!

"But call me if you want to talk selling options for the album."

"Okay." I hold back saying ten billion more things to him. They're within me, but I've got them simmering under a lid for the moment. My pot might runneth over around Ted lately, but I'm going to be a freaking rock star to Milo.

CHAPTER TWENTY-THREE

Places to Take Someone That Could Be Romantic, by Riley

1. <u>VIP Lounge at the Troubadour</u>
   I've never been up there and I want to! It looks like they have couches, so you could sit with someone on a couch and feel important and exclusive together. (I am against PDA, though, so no kissing or whatever else on the couch.)

2. <u>Secret room in the school no one knows about</u>
   I don't know if Edendale has any of these, but if so it would be pretty sexy sneaking off to it to make out with someone.

3. Hike in Altadena
   I went here on a field trip once. There's
   a waterfall you could stand behind to make
   out and no one would know you were there.
4. Your own room
   Duh.

CHAPTER TWENTY-FOUR

Reid cannot believe the story of Milo the handwriter.

"I can't believe that guy did that!" he says as we walk to English lit.

I didn't call him last night because I was basking in the glow of having been hit on. Also, homework. This is our first chance to talk today since he got to school late because of a dentist appointment. Reid's really into his dental hygiene. "He just did that!"

"*You're* the one who said people go there to meet people," I say. "And he gave me his number. He didn't have sex with me in the store or something."

"Still! I could never do that. I am not That Guy."

"No one said you were."

"If I were That Guy..." Reid shakes his head. "Everything would be different."

"Okay," I say because Reid is making this all about him, and I do not like it. "Anyway—"

"Like, how did he do it?" He grabs my hand and scrutinizes

the ink that lightened but didn't disappear in the shower this morning. A scientific person might hypothesize I covered it with a shower cap, but luckily Reid is, in addition to not being That Guy, not a man of science.

"I literally just told you how he did it." I wait for him to ask if I'm going to call him, if I'm interested, if I safely wrote the number down already, how it made me feel to have That Guy show me he's interested.

"I would already be going out with Jane if I was That Guy," he says.

"Maybe Jane's not into That Guy." I'm not sure I'm into That Guy, after all.

"No, every girl's into That Guy," he says, as if he speaks for all of womankind.

"What guy?" Lucy walks up to us like she's been part of the conversation all along.

"I have to go," I say, even though Reid and I are walking to the same place. I walk past Garrick, but I don't know what to say thanks to Sydney Jacobs, so I just fake a smile and keep moving.

"Hey." Reid catches up with me. "What's up?"

"You devoted, like, a fifth of the pages in the Passenger Manifest to one interaction with Jane," I say. "And you can't even pretend you're interested in this?"

It's a way more honest thing than I planned on saying.

"Shit," he says.

It makes me giggle because Reid hardly ever curses.

"Sorry," he says.

"No, it's okay. Do you think I should call him?"

"Yes," he says, with conviction.

"Really?"

"Ri, *yes*. Even if he's the worst person ever, you get to call That Guy."

He's right, and I know it, so after a respectable wait after school (two hours and twenty-seven minutes) I call.

"Hello."

"Hi, is this Milo?" It's kind of a dumb question because I can tell it's him and also who else would it be?

"Yeah, who's this?"

"This is, um..." And if you're going to stumble over anything, really, your own name? "Riley. We met yesterday at—"

"Giving up that album that easy?"

"No way," I say really quickly.

"I didn't peg you as a girl who would hand over an awesome album. So, you maybe want to hang out sometime?" he asks.

I try to think of a subtle way to ask how old he is.

"Maybe," I say, stalling. Also because it's true. Maybe I do, maybe I don't. Crap, I sound like the Riddler. Only in my head, but that is bad enough. "How old are you?"

That is the least subtle way possible.

"Eighteen," he says. "You?"

"Sixteen and a half," I say, because totally mature people still use halves.

WHY DID I SAY THAT?

"Okay then," he says.

"You can laugh," I say. "That was weird."

"We should hang out," he says. "What are you doing Thursday?"

"Band practice," I say. "Friday?"

"Band practice," he says, and my heart blossoms into ten million vases of the most beautiful daisies. "What do you play?"

"Drums." I picture us loading up our music-playing babies into an old VW bus and touring the country like the Partridge Family, which I definitely don't watch on TV Land whenever it runs, no way, not me.

"Yeahhh," he says, like an endorsement.

I decide it can only mean that he too had flashes of 1970s musical-family togetherness.

"What about you?"

"Tuba."

What is he talking about? "What?" The idea refuses to gel in my head.

"*Marching* band practice," he says.

"Oh." I try my best not to say it like a beloved family member just kicked the bucket.

"Marching band's cool," he says. "C'mon. The tuba is awesome."

I laugh before I can stop myself. Milo, don't think I'm a jerk! It's just that you look way more like a guitar than a tuba!

"You just have no idea," he says.

I can tell through his voice that he's smiling, so I guess he doesn't mind that I laughed. "How about I call you on Saturday, see how the weekend looks. Cool?"

"Yup," I say, which means we've spoken twice, and I've *yup*ped twice. Guh-reat.

But it's not like Milo's exactly as cool as he seems, either.

CHAPTER TWENTY-FIVE

Reid's Advice for Girls on How to Get Guys to Like You

1. Listen to good music.
2. Don't be ugly.
3. Don't spend a lot of time complaining publicly. It's grating.
4. Flirt with me, but not too much or it's suspicious.
5. Understand that guys have no idea what they're doing so just go with it.
6. Don't act like my mom.
7. Don't ask me to dance.

Riley's Advice for Guys on How to Get Girls to Like You

1. Listen to good music.
2. Don't be boring.
3. Have good hair.

CHAPTER TWENTY-SIX

I forget to turn my phone on vibrate during practice on Saturday, and between songs I hear it ring. I'm sure it's Milo, and it's like a straight shot of caffeine. Once we're onto the next song, I throw some showy stuff into my last run-through of the new fill. My sticks pummel the snare, capped off by a few extra accents on the sixteenth notes. It ends in a buzz that vibrates my teeth.

Reid notices, because Reid notices everything you don't want him to.

"Fancy," he says once the song's over.

So, "Fancy," I chipmunk back at him.

"Do you need to check that?" Lucy says because outside of the matter of honesty she's the nicest person in the world.

"No, it can wait," I say with as much Most Casual Attitude Ever imbued into those four words as I can manage. "We need to really nail 'Riverside Drive.' The fall formal is, like, any day."

"Riley's right," Nathan says.

"Yeah, your family's one thing," Reid says. "The whole school…"

The four of us stare at each other like we've just realized there are ten billion ways this could go wrong.

"Guys, we're going to rock," I say, like it wasn't me who just started the *HEY-LET'S-PANIC-THE-DANCE-IS-AROUND-THE-CORNER* train speeding down the tracks. "The whole of Edendale High isn't going to judge us, except on a scale of awesome."

"I love the scale of awesome," Lucy says. "Riley's right. Let's just get serious, and it'll go great."

"I'm always serious!" Reid says, which is true.

"It'll be great. We can do this," I say.

We play through "Riverside Drive" a few more times, move on to "Incandescent," and finish up with our cover of Ted Leo's "Me and Mia." I try to put myself in the mind space of a typical Edendale student and take us in like we're brand-new.

Reid's bass is solid, an unrepentant throbbing rhythm pulling us all into a connection. More and more lately, the beats and the crashes and the thrum of my sticks sound bigger than me and also somehow totally me at once. Nathan's and Lucy's vocals are sweet and salty together, like maple bacon ice cream, somewhere between 1960s dreamboats and back when Jenny and Blake still happily sang together in Rilo Kiley and something that's uniquely us.

After practice I discover something that ruins any chance of my new amazing casual attitude lasting any longer: the missed call and voice mail are totally not from Milo. They are from Sydney Jacobs–doer, Garrick, and I think of his shaggy hair and his science/kissing skills, and I smile, and then I think of Sydney Jacobs again, and I turn that smile upside down.

"That Guy?" Reid asks me.

"I wouldn't say that." I'm not going for vaguely mysterious but somehow pull it off anyway. I start to explain, but it'll go into the Passenger Manifest later. So I wait until I'm alone in my car to listen to Garrick's voice mail.

"Hi, Riley, it's Garrick Bell. Your chemistry partner."

HOW IS GARRICK A GENIUS WHEN HE SAYS THINGS LIKE THIS?

"I just wanted to see if you were doing anything. Probably you're going to a cool underground secret show at the Smell tonight."

HOW DOES GARRICK KNOW ABOUT THE SMELL?

"But if you're free, I was thinking about hanging out, maybe seeing a movie at the Vista. Okay, talk to you later, or not, I guess see you Monday otherwise. Bye!"

I don't know what this means. If this were a normal guy, I'd consider this an ask-out, which would make hanging out a date. But of course it seems I don't even know any normal guys, because while I was figuring out if a scientific genius was an okay sort for a rock star (in training) to date, I was now struggling with figuring out if a lowly civilian was an okay sort for a celebrity-sex-haver to date. Or even just make out with.

After all, I still want to make out with Garrick. Even if Ted Callahan reigns supreme as the Crush and even if I might have plans at some point in my life with Milo, That Guy.

I call Garrick as I'm driving home.

"Hey, Garrick, it's Riley."

"Hi, did you just have practice? I remembered right after I left you a message."

"Yeah, but it's cool. When do you want to hang out?"

"I don't know, soon? And great! Do you want to meet me here? My house, I mean. Or there? The Vista, I mean. You know what I mean, so I don't know why I just explained both of those."

"I can meet you at your house."

"Great." He sounds like he means that.

He lets me in right away when I get to his house, and his parents are clearly out, so instead of talking about chemistry or going to a movie, it's an instant smush of our faces together, right there in the Bells' front room, like we can't wait a second longer. It always sounded exaggerated in songs, but now that I was in this moment, I *couldn't* wait a second longer.

"Hey," I say, because I feel there are matters to clear up, even though my hands are buried deep in Garrick's perfectly shaggy and well-conditioned hair while his have settled at the small of my back, under my shirt, on my bare skin. I had no idea it could feel good for someone to touch *your back*.

"Sorry," he says, professional and polite, pulling back from me.

I see that he thinks it has something to do with the skin-on-skin contact, and I want to fix that misunderstanding right away, but if I jump right back into kissing him there will still be matters to clear up.

"No," I say, "it's just, you know, the whole thing, is all, not you, not your hands, I mean, that's all."

Jeez, Riley, five billion vague phrases does not a sentence make.

"Are you okay?" He probably thinks I just had a stroke.

"I don't smell any burnt toast, if that's what you're wondering."

Garrick stares at me as blankly as a boy genius can.

"You know, they say you smell toast if you have a stroke."

MORE BLANK STARING.

"I didn't have a stroke is what I'm saying."

"I'm glad we cleared that up." He laughs and goes off to get us some sodas. It's fancy root beer made with real sugar, bottled in Mexico, where all the good sodas come from. "Are you okay?"

"I know about Sydney Jacobs," I say.

"Oh, right. I guess I figured you would have already known. Anyway, it's over between us," he says, the way people talk on television when they've had Life Experience. "Were you reading Nick Gossip dot com? I heard that blog said something about Syd not ending things with 'an old flame.'"

I picture Garrick as a candle in the wind, and I almost laugh, but then my gut registers the intimate *Syd.*

"I believe you," I say, "and I wasn't reading Nick Gossip dot com. Just—she's famous."

"Kind of," he says.

"And I'm not."

He cocks his head. "So?"

I can't figure out how to say I'm a nobody without sounding like I want assurance that I'm not.

"Riley," he says, like my whole name is a sigh.

"Let's go to a movie," I say finally.

"Great." He seems relieved that I changed the subject.

"Sorry," I say.

"It's okay." Garrick is suddenly made of kindness and understanding, in addition to shaggy hair and crazy good lips. "Ready to go?"

"Totally." We walk over to Hillhurst and then down to the Vista and absolutely no more making out happens, not during the movie, not during the dark walk back to his house later.

CHAPTER TWENTY-SEVEN

<u>The Sad Animal Project, Continued, by Reid</u>

I stop by Paws for People "randomly" (Jane had mentioned that her schedule rarely changes) and act like I'm surprised to see her there. I remember to give a lot of attention to the one-eyed dog supposedly meant for me. Jane asks me if I asked my parents about the dog yet, and even though I know I originally did say "parents" I correct her and say "my mom, actually" and tell her how my parents are divorced and my dad lives in Chicago now.

Jane looks really guilty she said it so I'm psyched I'm getting sympathy out of this!

She's the only one working again, so I hang out with her and help walk dogs, and something really amazing happens. At one point she makes this sad face and I ask her if she's okay. And she says the greatest thing a girl has ever said about me.

"I was just thinking once you bring home the dog you won't come in to help me so much!"

So I tell her it might be a while after all before I can adopt the dog, and also maybe after I do I can still come by to help her out, or I'll at least see her around. I tried to say it all smooth like "seeing you around" means "going out with you" but I'm not sure I did it right. I am not That Guy.

I stay until Paws for People is closed, and I ask Jane if she wants to hang out. She says she can't because she made plans already. It's pretty disappointing but I handle it like a pro. Actually I guess if the topic is "having girls make excuses not to hang out with you" I _am_ a pro. But this time I don't think it's an excuse, I'm at least 85 percent sure it's true.

CHAPTER TWENTY-EIGHT

Once I'm home that night, in my pajamas watching TV in the living room because Mom and Dad think it's harmful to your brain development or your psyche or your vision to have a TV in your own bedroom, I listen to a new voice mail from Milo.

"Hey, Riley, it's Milo. Call me. Later."

It's late—like, infomercials-are-playing-abundantly-across-multiple-cable-networks late—so I don't, but after a weird night with Garrick, it's good to have Milo waiting in the wings.

Wait. *The wings?* My life is a play with a bunch of dude understudies?

Actually that sounds awesome.

Dad walks downstairs into the room. "What are you still doing up?"

"I'm sixteen," I say. "And it isn't that late."

"I guess not," he says. "Want some popcorn?"

"We have popcorn? Yes."

"I won't reveal where," he says, disappearing into the kitchen, "but I have a hiding place."

I'm too lazy to get up, so I don't solve the mystery of where in the world is the secret popcorn. Also this acne-treatment infomercial is finally starting to get interesting.

"Voilà," Dad says, coming back into the room with a bowl of popcorn, yay, and a shaker of Parmesan cheese, double yay.

"Awesome." I stare at the TV as teenagers get their lives back. Apparently there are no lives with zits. "Did you have a lot of girlfriends in high school?"

Dad kind of laughs. "Well, yeah."

Well, yeah?

"College, too." He grins and takes a huge handful of popcorn. He needs sustenance to relish these lady memories. Ew. "Until I met your mom, of course."

"Dad, I know." I wish we could have this conversation without my having to think about Dad having dozens of girlfriends. "Just—that's okay, right?"

"What do you mean?"

"Like, I don't know. Knowing a lot of people."

" 'Knowing'? Or dating?"

WHY AM I ASKING MY DAD ABOUT THIS? "Never mind."

"I'm just trying to figure out what you're saying," Dad says. "But of course it's fine. As long as you aren't in committed relationships."

Committed relationships sound like they're for people so old they worry about taxes and retirement plans and laxatives.

"Did you ever like three girls at once?" I ask, even though I don't really want the answer.

"Well, yeah," he says, again, "of course."

OF COURSE?

Instead of dwelling on that, I turn my attention back to the on-screen teens and their miraculous better-skin miracles. And I decide I will call Milo tomorrow and see Ted Monday at school and figure out what the heck is up with Garrick and enjoy the fact there are suddenly so many options. I am not Reid with his weird rankings and back-up plans. I just like these guys.

*   *   *

There's all sorts of noise in the background when Milo answers the phone on late Sunday morning.

"Hey," he says.

"What's going on there?" I ask. "Band practice?"

"Ha-ha," he says. "I'm mowing the lawn."

"You can call me back later if you want."

"I'm talking to you now, right?" he says with a laugh. "What are you doing today?"

"I'm not sure yet," I say. "What are you doing, besides lawn mowing?"

"I'm not sure yet, either. Want to hang out?"

I suddenly feel like it's weird. I don't even know this guy, other than his first name and his phone number and that he plays the tuba and has good taste in music and that he's eighteen. And now we could just *hang out?*

I guess that's what dating is.

"Sure," I say, doing my best to sound like this is standard operating procedure for me.

"Where do you live?" he asks. "I'm in Eagle Rock. We can pick a halfway spot."

"I'm in Los Feliz," I say. "Do you want to look at music at Jacknife Records in Atwater Village? And we can go to the farmers' market and get free fruit samples and eat *pupusas*?"

Wow, I am suddenly brimming with ideas. Who knew!

"That sounds good," he says. "Meet at twelve thirty?"

That doesn't give me a ton of time to transform from Pajama Self to Normal Self, but I agree with this earlier-than-I'd-like time since he agreed with my agenda for the day. I was hoping dating would all be about hanging out and making out, but apparently there is also going to be compromise.

Milo is waiting at the entrance to the farmers' market when I walk up, and he is like a vision, with his blond hair glowing in the sun and his Deerhoof T-shirt and his green Chuck Taylors and his jeans that I know would make his butt look awesome if he were to suddenly turn around. Milo, turn around!

"Hey," he greets me. He is really good at casual.

"Hey." I do an okay job myself, even without anywhere to lean.

"Come on." He nods to the farmers' market. "You said something about *pupusas*."

"Totally, I did." I walk in, past the booths selling fresh produce and organic homemade scented candles and fancy goat cheese, and get in line, with Milo right behind me. I always get really excited about getting *pupusas*, the fattest, most delicious corn tortillas stuffed with deliciousness, specifically beans and cheese and veggies and meat and whatever else, and topped with slaw and salsa and sour cream. Serious heaven.

"So how's that Sandwiches album working out for you?" Milo asks.

"It hasn't left my car stereo since I got it," I say. "The sound is amazing, whatever they did remastering it."

"Man, I never care about sound," he says. "I feel like some of the best stuff's recorded on crappy equipment in some dude's basement, and it doesn't matter."

"It doesn't *have* to matter," I say, "but when it's something amazing, and then the sound's great, too, it's, like, synergy."

Milo laughs, and I know I haven't convinced him. It's fine; I don't need a frigging tuba player to back my music opinions.

"What kind do you want?" Milo asks me, stepping up to order.

"Two bean and cheese." I don't love the thing where because Milo's a guy he's supposed to pay, so I get a five out of my purse and hand it to him. He doesn't act like that's odd, so points gained for Milo.

We take our food and strawberry lemonades to the nearby picnic tables and, thanks to the crowd, end up sitting side by side.

"So what's your band like?" Milo asks me.

"Kind of sixties garage pop is the best description, I

115

guess," I say. "I don't always like saying who we're like, since I hope we're our own thing? But when I do, like, Smith Westerns, Best Coast, maybe, like, Rilo Kiley before they sold out." I reach into my bag and take out one of our buttons from the Ziploc baggie that's always with me. "This is us, if you want to go to our website; we have some demos and stuff."

"Cool," he says, examining the button and putting it into his pocket. "You guys need a tuba?"

"Not so much." I take a sip of my lemonade. "Why did you get started playing the tuba anyway?"

"Some guy came to our school when I was in fifth grade or whatever with all these instruments and talked them up, and I thought the tuba was the shit. And I just kept playing. I'm good at it, so..." He laughs and shrugs.

"Is your band marching?" I ask.

"Yeah, I'm in marching band, and I'm in orchestra, too."

"Do you want to, like, play professional tuba someday?"

"I don't know." He takes a few huge bites of *pupusa*, which is liberally drenched in salsa. "I'm not really thinking ahead to that point yet. My teacher wants me to apply to Juilliard and all."

"Seriously? You're all blasé about applying to *Juilliard*?"

"I don't think we should be making life decisions now," he says.

I shrug. "Unless you know. I totally know what I want to do with my life."

"Be a drummer?"

"Be a rock star," I say. "I mean—you know, be in a band, be a serious musician, whatever."

"You mean *be a rock star*," he says with a huge grin.

I decide he isn't patronizing me, and grin back.

"You ready to go sample some fruit?"

"No, hang on, I'm still eating," I say with a nod to my paper plate.

"Are you going to the Vanderbilts show on Tuesday?" he asks.

"It's not an all-ages show," I say, my least favorite sentence about concerts, ever. Right before *There's a Ticketmaster charge.* "Are you secretly twenty-one?"

"No, but I have ID that says I am." He looks at me like I'm an idiot. "You're this into music and you don't have an ID? We have to take care of that," he says. "You miss out on way too much otherwise."

"*I KNOW!*" I say more loudly than necessary. Take it easy, Riley. "I'm always missing amazing shows."

"I know a guy," he says, which I love, because isn't that always how shady stuff goes down. "We'll take care of it."

"*OH MY GOD!*" My volume is turned up way too loud again. "In time to see the Vanderbilts on Tuesday?"

"Yeah, we'll make it happen."

After I finish my lunch, we toss our trash and wander around the tiny farmers' market, sampling strawberries, plums, peaches, and passion fruit, before heading down Glendale Boulevard to Jacknife Records.

"Whoa," Milo says when we're prowling around Jacknife. "Check it out."

It's a copy of the Sandwiches album. "You'd better get it before another person moves faster than you do."

"Then I guess I'll have no reason to talk to you again," he says with a grin. It's such a good grin.

"I guess not," I say. "It's all I have to offer to the world."

He buys the CD and texts the guy who apparently has the fate of my seeing the Vanderbilts in his hands. And we get coffee—well, chai—at Kaldi, and I find out we have seemingly countless favorite bands in common. Milo tells me about the time he met Kim Deal of the Breeders and the Pixies at a Coffee Bean & Tea Leaf. I tell him about the time I tripped down the sidewalk because Dee Dee Penny of Dum Dum Girls walked by, but it's not nearly as good a story, and we both know it.

And hopefully I'm not being unfair to Ted—or Garrick—to think that this is actually how a rock star should fall in love.

CHAPTER TWENTY-NINE

<u>The Sad Animal Project, Continued, by Reid</u>

I stop by Paws again, but it seems okay and not like I'm a stalker because the dad-type guy says something about how people always want to hang out with their dogs once they've picked them. Also it's really late, almost time for them to close, and I act distracted like I don't know what time it is. Jane giggles like it's cute that I didn't know. So I hang around until they have to close up, and I guess when her boss is there I can't help her, so I tell her I can wait for her if she wants.

And she says she does want.

She asks if I want to hang out because she's free and it was fun last time. I try to play it cool but I probably seem pretty eager, but it's okay since technically she's the one doing the asking, so I'm in.

I try to think of awesome places to suggest but my mind's completely blank. Luckily Jane suggests we see a movie, which is great. She wants to see this foreign animated film, which doesn't exactly sound like a good date movie to me but it's great she's so interesting and also that she doesn't want to see something inherently crappy. It's playing at The Los Feliz 3 so it takes us a while to find parking but we're good on time, and when we get to the theater she lets me buy her ticket and popcorn and soda, so it's clear this is a date. It's got to be, with the buying of stuff, right?

The movie's actually pretty good, and at one point it gets kind of sad--though I don't cry or anything--but I can tell Jane's getting kind of emotional, and I kind of nudge her to see if she's okay and she gives me the best smile and then leans her head on my shoulder.

Unfortunately the movie is almost over! We do sit through the credits so that's really good, though at some point during them she sits up all the way and stretches, so that's over. I have to go to the bathroom really badly but I don't want to lose momentum so I just walk out of the theater with her and ask if she wants to go to House of Pies or Fred 62. She checks her phone and says she should probably actually get home so if I could just drive her back to her car that would be great.

So I do, and the whole way I'm getting up the nerve to kiss her, but the best I can do is ask if she's going to the fall formal. She says she is, to see us play!!

Okay, then, something can happen at the dance. It's all lining up.

CHAPTER THIRTY

Reid is waiting by my locker on Monday morning, and I am 99.9 percent sure it's because I left the Passenger Manifest for him in our secret spot (i.e., my house's mailbox on Sunday nights because no one ever looks there) last night. I'd detailed my date or whatever it was with Milo pretty fully.

"He's getting you an ID?" Reid waves his hands around for, I guess, emphasis. It looks like he's attempting to land a plane in the hallway. "Riley! Do you know how long I've wanted an ID?"

I maneuver past him to get into my locker. "No, I don't know how long you've wanted an ID. A while?"

"Yes, a while. I can't believe you didn't think to ask for me, too. Who are you going to shows with if I can't go? Or Lucy or Nathan?"

"Um, Milo? I thought that was pretty obvious."

"Fine." Reid scowls. "See you later."

If I were him, I'd probably be jealous, too. But considering

Milo's doing me a huge favor, I feel weird asking if he'll get an ID for Reid, too.

Ted rounds the corner. "Hey, Riley."

"Hey! How was your weekend? Did you do anything fun?" I say in the overly loud voice that seems reserved for all interactions with Ted.

"Not really. Just boring stuff. What about you?"

"Band practice; besides that, the same," I say, because it doesn't feel right to talk about Garrick or Milo in front of Ted. Obviously.

"See you in Spanish?" he asks.

"Well, yeah, and in history class first." I smile at him because oh my god it's cute you sort of made a mistake, Ted. "And if you need a ride tonight, I'm totally free after school."

"Thanks," he says, and takes off down the hallway.

Just then Lucy walks up to me. "You're always talking to him lately," she says.

I'm surprised that she's noticed but also thrilled! Ted and I talk enough that it seems like *always*. "I guess, kind of."

"Because of Yearbook?" she asks. "Or is it something else?"

"What do you mean?" I ask. "Homework?"

"No!" Lucy laughs and glances around like she's making sure no one's listening. "Is something up with him? Something"—she grins and raises her eyebrows—"sexy?"

Lucy would have made the exact same joke pre-Nathan, *I KNOW THIS*, but now it's different. And I don't know how to answer because nothing specifically sexy is up with him, but

I have to believe Ted and I are maybe in our phase of witty repartee that's headed directly to more straightforward sexy things. So I just shrug and leave it at that.

I sit down next to Garrick in chemistry, and he smiles at me in a manner I believe to be beyond our old level of Chemistry Partner Friendliness. Considering the rapid decline in amount of making out on Saturday night, I'm happy to see this.

"Hi," he says. "Are you busy tonight?"

Whoa! This is unexpected.

"Actually I am," I say. "I have a thing." Probably the possibility that maybeI'lldriveTedtohismom'sofficeafterschool doesn't actually qualify as *a thing*, but it's what I've got.

"Oh, okay." He glances around just like Lucy did, checking for any eavesdroppers. "It's really over with Sydney. If you didn't believe me, I promise it's true."

"No, I...I believe you. I was just surprised by the whole you-dating-a-TV-star thing. Maybe we can hang out later this week?"

"Yeah, I'm free almost every night." He shakes his head. "I sound like a loser. It's just not a busy week."

"I get it," I say. "I have Yearbook and band and Family Night, but I'll figure something out. We should definitely hang out."

After school I hover near Ted's locker in the hallway. He smiles when he heads over.

"Hey, Riley," he says. "Thanks for waiting."

"No problem," I say.

We're quiet as we walk to my car, but it feels normal and not bad for Ted to be quiet, so I don't panic. When I start the car, the volume of the Titus Andronicus CD in my stereo is up way louder than I remember it being this morning, and my hand flies over to the volume almost automatically to prevent Ted and me from both being deafened.

"What band is this?" Ted asks instead of saying "Now I will never make out with you because you almost took the sound out of my life forever," which is what I'm expecting.

"Titus Andronicus," I say.

"Oh, I think I saw them at FYF Fest over the summer," he says. "Did you?"

"No! My parents picked that week for family vacation, so I was exploring Colonial Williamsburg instead." I'm still annoyed I'd been off dipping wicks in wax to make sad misshapen candles instead of seeing a ton of amazing bands.

"It was kind of lame, actually," Ted says. "Not the music, which was cool, even though I didn't really know any of the bands."

He didn't really know any of the bands? *HE DIDN'T REALLY KNOW ANY OF THE BANDS?*

"But it was out in this park without any shade, and it took me an hour waiting in line to get this kind of gross tuna sandwich to eat. I'm still glad my cousin took me, though."

"Yeah, my friend Reid went; he said the same thing, except

for the tuna sandwich part. I did learn about churning butter at least."

Ted laughs, this actual laugh like I am an actual hilarious person. I forgive him for not being as cool about music as I'd suspected. "My mom went there once when she was little. She's always telling us about it like she actually time traveled. It's a little weird."

"It's kind of like that, to be fair to your mom," I say, and wonder if it's okay to defend Ted's mom to him.

Why can't I think of anything else to say now? We're not quite to his mom's office yet. I have talking time. I have Make Ted Fall In Love With Me time. Whyyyy aren't I using it wisely? Riley, get it together. Say something. Keep Ted in the car as long as possible.

"They also make wigs!" I exclaim.

Ted stares at me. "What?"

"In Colonial Williamsburg," I say. "That's all."

"Oh."

We are quiet until I pull up to his mom's office building. And I have earned every single painful time-bending moment that ticks by.

CHAPTER THIRTY-ONE

<u>The Vanderbilts Show, by Riley</u>

I meet Milo in front of the Echo on Tuesday night, and when I'm walking up to him I'm crazy nervous he won't actually have the ID, but once I see him I forget FOR JUST A MOMENT because he looks exactly like the kind of guy who'd hang out all casual in front of the Echo. He's wearing a Daft Punk T-shirt and a stripey cardigan that wouldn't look good on most guys, but most guys are not Milo.

(Yes, Reid, what I'm saying is, I'm not sure cardigans are for you.)

And then...it happens! He gives me what completely looks like a real California driver's license proclaiming my name is Jennifer Anne Matthews. I try to be casual like a rock star but I can't help leaping around a little while thanking him.

We go to Two Boots for pizza, since we have time before the show starts. I pay for our slices (I know you'll ask, so the answer is, we each get a piece of the Newman and of the Dude), since Milo won't take money for the ID, and it's the nicest thing I can think to do.

We talk about the last shows we've seen (Milo: Modern Marvel, me: Bleached) and upcoming shows we're playing (Milo: his school's football game Friday night, me: the fall formal).

After we eat, we walk back to the Echo and show our IDs (!!!) to the bouncer, who lets us right through. Probably I should have been nervous about that whole transaction, but luckily I forgot to be because Milo was being so cool about everything and I guess it rubbed off on me. Once we're inside I feel superprivileged to be here on a night when no one else my age should be. (Sorry, Reid, but it's true.)

Milo asks if I want a beer, and I accidentally blurt out, "You can get us beers?" I'm shocked, but then I remember fake IDs do more than get you into shows you are dying to see. They're multipurpose! So we each have a beer, and we find an excellent spot to stand near the stage. As you know, the best spot is right between the amps and speakers, but where I still have a good view of the drummer. Also where a tall dude can't stand in front of me, because it seems amazing how tall dudes always come to the same shows I do and manage to find the one open space in front of me.

While Stool Boom, the first opener, is setting up, Milo says: "I listened to your demo tracks. I can pick out drums. You're really good."

It is maybe the best thing a guy's ever said to me ever.

Stool Boom is okay, nothing special, but the next opener, Sweetpants, is a better fit with the Vanderbilts. Of course the Vanderbilts are incredible, and Milo is a great fellow concertgoer. He makes a lot of noise, and we both nod to the beat.

I don't want to sound like a cheeseball like you, Reid, but it is a pretty perfect night.

CHAPTER THIRTY-TWO

I make a scary discovery the next morning when I'm brushing my teeth. Kissing Milo—who's maybe a little bitey—has resulted in a swollen lower lip. I can't tell if it's obvious but I feel like it's a blinking light on my face. I convince myself it's in my head and finish getting ready, but Ashley stares as we walk out to my car together.

"What's wrong with your lip?" she asks.

"I ran into someone," I say, which doesn't make sense, so I add, "someone's face, I mean." *WHICH MAKES EVEN LESS SENSE, THOUGH IT IS ALSO SORT OF TRUE.*

Ashley eyes me like I'm crazy.

I drop Ashley off at the middle school and make the fastest Starbucks run ever because between the late night and the swollen lip and the beer, my body and brain are not exactly ready for education. I speed to school and run inside like it's the LA Marathon, even though back during freshman year when I had to take gym I wouldn't run unless I got called out by Coach Gunderson to do so.

I still get stopped at the entrance to the school and get a tardy slip. At first I panic, but anything I miss in chemistry Garrick will cover for, and also maybe I am cementing myself as some kind of badass with a swollen lip and coffee I'm sneaking in carefully in my backpack and now this tardy slip.

"Hey, Riley."

I wonder if Ted's voice is a sleep deprivation–induced apparition. I'm not expecting anyone else to be in the hallway after the bell, much less Ted Callahan, and I trip on absolutely nothing and slam into a locker. The coffee in my backpack of course doesn't remain upright throughout this, and suddenly, hot brown liquid spews out the bottom.

"Whoa." Ted dashes over. "Is your bag leaking? Sorry, obviously it's leaking. What just happened?"

"I was trying to sneak in coffee in my backpack," I sort of wail, yanking open the backpack's zipper and extracting all my stuff. Ted runs into the guys' bathroom and returns a moment later with a ton of paper towels. We manage to dry off my textbooks, but my chemistry notebook is pretty damp and discolored.

"Thanks," I tell Ted, who is cool in a liquid emergency. "I can't believe that just happened."

"Me neither!" He laughs and takes all the wet paper towels to the bathroom to throw away.

I expect he'll rush off to wherever he was heading, late, as well, but he just comes back calmly to me. It's the only time in recent history we've stood this close and I haven't wanted to kiss him, thanks to my stupid lip.

"You should get to class," I tell him.

"No, I have a free period this hour," he says. "Well, actually I'm Ms. Matteson's aide but she normally doesn't have a lot for me to do, so it's more like study hall. Where are you going to put your bag? You should let it dry out somewhere."

"I don't know," I say glumly.

"I'll take it to her classroom." Ted points down the hallway. "You can pick it up after seventh period. Cool?"

"Supercool," I say, because I am the dorkiest person alive. "Thank you, seriously. You're like a hero."

Ted laughs again. It's so great to hear. I wish we were the kind of close where I could just reach over and give him the kind of hug where you bury yourself into the other person. Okay, actually I guess even with my lip in its sad state I'm back to thinking about kissing, et cetera.

"I should go to class at least," I say. "See you later. And, seriously, thanks."

He waves as he walks off. "Anytime."

* * *

Lucy and I are discussing our algebra homework at my locker after chemistry when Garrick walks by and waves. I manage a supercasual wave back like this is No Big Thing.

"Did you know Garrick used to go out with some girl who's on a kids' show?" Lucy asks once he's passed by. "Isn't it crazy?"

It is crazy, but also I guess I've been swayed by the gospel of tween bloggers because it's less crazy all the time.

"Yeah, I know. I guess it's not crazy, though." I shrug. "Garrick's cute if you forget how he loves science, I think."

It's dangerously close to admitting something, but I feel I have to stick up for Garrick on the subject of his celebrity-having-sex-with worthiness.

"Hmm," Lucy says, watching Garrick walk down the hallway away from us.

I can tell she's considering it. It would be a great time to explain how I know firsthand that Garrick's make-out abilities could probably bring about world peace if he was sent to the right places. But I don't, and Lucy heads off, and I walk quickly to catch up with Garrick before he heads into class.

"Hey, what are you doing tonight?" he asks me.

"Nothing," I say, because the coffee and my medicated lip balm are working. Kissing sounds *great* again! "Do you want to hang out?"

"Yes," he says, and grins. Hopefully he's not getting all excited about the prospect of studying like good little chemists but is instead calculating how much making out is possible with me.

* * *

Garrick has flash cards in his hand when he lets me in after school, but I lean in to kiss him, and there's no hesitation on his part.

We lean back against the door, and I feel like my whole

body's buzzing because Garrick is pressed up against me, like, fully pressed up against me. His hands are holding my face, which I find straight-out-of-a-good-romantic-comedy romantic.

"Riley," Garrick says, and I am expecting him to declare his love for me.

"Yeah?" I ask, slipping my hand up his T-shirt, but not trying to make my voice sexy because I can only really handle one of those seduction techniques at once.

"We really should study," he says.

"Oh," I say.

"The test coming up is really important," he says. "And I'm applying for this student volunteer opportunity at UCLA, and I want Mr. Landiss to have no room to say anything negative about me."

"I get it," I say, because despite that I was really hoping studying would not come into play today, I do get it. The Gold Diggers have been practicing more than usual to get ready for our gig at the fall formal, and I guess to science geeks a test is a lot like a gig. So we sit on the couch and get out our notebooks and textbooks. Garrick gets us fancy sodas and a bag of organic Parmesan-flavored chips. A couple of weeks ago, this is what I would have expected from a study session with Garrick, but now it's a total letdown.

Maybe it's Sydney Jacobs. Or maybe it really is that science is more important to Garrick than sex. Well, things-leading-up-to-sex, at least. I try to quickly calculate if music or things-leading-up-to-sex are more important to me.

"Hey," I say, kind of out of nowhere. "Do you want to go to the Andrew Mothereffing Jackson show with me? It's next week at the Satellite."

"Who's that?" he asks.

My hope that Garrick is secretly some kind of music nerd because he's heard of the Smell and once selected a good album on my iPod flickers a bit.

"A local band, but they tour nationally and stuff. They're just these really loud punk guys, but they have kind of this 1960s vibe, the whole perfect three-chord song thing, and their drummer's kind of crazy. Me and Reid always say he reminds us of Animal from the Muppets."

Garrick's looking at me pretty blankly, which is not an attractive expression on anyone, so I make a stern mental note to always at least pretend I know what the heck is going on if I ever want to get past second base with anyone.

"You're probably busy," I say, to save both of us. Have I decided we need saving? Yes, yes, we do. "With your application for this UCLA thing."

"Yeah, I really am," he says.

"Cool," I say, even though I'm feeling really uncool. "Hey, um, so, can I ask you something? I'm kind of embarrassed about it, but…"

"But?" Garrick asks.

"But I'm just going to ask it. Okay. Did you and Sydney Jacobs ever…you know…do it?"

"That's really personal," he says.

"Oh, okay," I say, like an understanding person. "You don't have to tell me."

"No, I can tell you," he says. "Yeah, we did. Don't tell anyone. I don't want anyone gossiping about her."

"Totally won't," I say, even though I'm going to write it down in the Passenger Manifest later. That doesn't count. Also maybe people in Ashley's circle would care that Sydney Jacobs had sex, but I don't think anyone in high school is exactly following Nickelodeon scandalous behavior.

"Let's get back to our flash cards," he says. And right now that does sound like the right call.

CHAPTER THIRTY-THREE

<u>Best Places for Doing It, by Riley</u>

1. <u>Your own bed (when your parents are away, obviously)</u>
   It's boring but free, and probably the most comfortable place.
2. <u>The guy's bed (when his parents are away, double obviously)</u>
   It's slightly less boring (for me) but also free and comfortable.
3. <u>Backstage at a concert (after, not during--don't disrespect live music)</u>
   I'll just say I've thought about this a lot.
4. <u>On a tour bus (parked, not in motion)</u>
   If no one else is around. I may have thought about this a lot, too.

Best Places for Doing It, by Reid (Fine, Ri, I will make this list even though I will probably never need it.)

1. <u>A fancy hotel</u>
   I'm not saying I can afford a fancy hotel, but I could save up or figure something out. If you're wanting to make the moment really special and romantic, this is your best option.

2. <u>A really nice house</u>
   I'm not sure how I'll get access to a really nice house, and mine is pretty average, but I think you could blow a girl's mind if you walk her into a house that's really big or is designed by a famous architect or is near a beautiful landmark.

3. <u>An expensive car</u>
   Would it be too weird if I borrowed Mom's BMW for these purposes? (Maybe you shouldn't answer this, Ri—I can hear your answer already and it's not good.)

CHAPTER THIRTY-FOUR

I should be terrified the night of the fall formal, but I am a Rock Star. I'm wearing my Upset T-shirt over a long-sleeved sparkly gold shirt, with a denim skirt, striped tights, and my cherry-red Doc Martens. The Gold Diggers have been using our free time to practice, and Reid set up a recording the other night. Despite the crappiness of the sound quality, something that wasn't crappy was us.

We are ready.

We're some of the first to arrive at the gym. Kids from the Edendale Spirit Club are setting up tables with punch and bottled water, while chaperones look on like the mere act of beverage setup and distribution is more than a bunch of over-achieving teenagers can handle. I ignore them, even though I could go for some punch. I assume successful musicians don't get distracted by a drink made for kindergarteners.

"Whoa!" Nathan skids into a slide as he carries over a mic stand. "Be careful, guys, the floor is really slick."

"I'm fine." I point to my boots, which aren't just badass but tend to protect me from things like floor slickness.

"This is pretty cool, right?" Reid asks, like he knows it is, but also like he wants some props for getting us this gig. *AGAIN.* It's weird how a guy can simultaneously have the best and worst self-esteem of anyone I know.

"It's pretty cool," Lucy says with a big smile. She's wearing delicate blue flats that match her dress, and she also slides across the floor and crashes into Nathan. They laugh like all the fun in the world is shared between the two of them alone.

"Hi, everyone." Ms. Matteson, who is the head chaperone for the dance, makes her way over to us. "Here's how it'll work. A DJ's playing the first half, then you guys will play your set. Feel free to play an encore if it seems like you should. Got it?"

"Got it," Nathan says in his Natural Leader way.

I'm too stuck on the idea of our school chanting *encore, encore, encore, encore.*

"Can we do a sound check now?"

"Of course, have at it. We'll just want you to clear the area at eight when the dance officially begins."

I sit down at my drums and wait for Ms. Matteson to walk off before counting off so we can play through "Tease." The gym is not exactly an acoustical wonderland, but we make it work. Reid is blathering on, saying he's nervous about everyone seeing us and judging us, so we're back to that, and I pretend like I'm calm, even though by now of course this show is a big deal, and I wish I could guarantee it'll be perfect.

After the sound check, we head out to a little room off the gym, where I imagine the basketball team gets pep talks before going out to play because people have written all this GO LIONS! graffiti over the walls. Backstage at a lot of concert venues it's practically encouraged to sign your band's name when you're playing, but I resist.

We could probably attend the DJ'ed first part of the dance, but we're treating this a lot like a real gig—I guess it is a real gig. So we hang out and go over our set list until Ms. Matteson summons us to the stage. I climb behind my drums, wait for Nathan to introduce us (he *is* best at it), and count off for "Tease."

People are watching, or dancing, or nodding approvingly. There are of course some bored-looking seniors hanging around the punch bowl, but, whatever, the majority of the crowd is into it.

And they should be! Nathan and Lucy are nailing every single lyric, and even with the muddy gym acoustics, their guitars ring out bright and harmonious. Reid and I are lacing a rhythm that's vibrating through the slick floor. Better yet, it's not like it's the two of them and the two of us: The Gold Diggers are all four of us, and it's so good when I remember that.

For the first time in my own history I love absolutely everything about my high school, especially when I catch sight of someone between songs: good hair, a button-down shirt, nice pants, and Converse. Ted's at the punch bowl. I'm not sure if he can see me too well, but I use my rock star energy to summon up the best smile I've given anyone.

And he smiles back.

"Garage" goes just as well, and then we're on a roll, and everything is flowing. Lucy, Nathan, and Reid are moving around onstage with ease—yes, even Reid!—and I'm nearly jumping off of my stool with energy and excitement and, just, *music*.

After our Ted Leo cover and then "Longer Days" to close the set, we make a proper exit and crowd back into the little room that now feels too small to contain us. I don't care about Lucy and Nathan's relationship, and I don't care that Reid and I are not huggers-of-one-another. Right now there is so much hugging and high-fiving going around between the four of us, you'd think something bigger than a great set at a high school formal just happened.

"Oh my god." Lucy speaks in the kind of hushed whisper people use in church. "You guys, listen."

There's clapping and wooing and whistling. And it's for us. They want an encore.

The energy is feeding us, and our two encore songs, "Figuring You Out" and "Going On," have never sounded like this before. I know that a friend of Nathan's is filming the set, and I'm so glad we'll have proof this happened one magical night in a school gymnasium. I picture the footage rolling in our *Behind the Music*.

After the set is over we stick around onstage, drinking in

the applause and attention and also because Ms. Matteson had told us as we walked out our equipment had to be off the stage by the time the dance technically ended.

"Hey, Riley," Ted says from behind me.

I turn around and smile.

"Hey, Ted." My face is still hot from adrenaline and stage lights and the general climate of the gym, and I can't control the tidal wave of words smacking at the shores of my mouth. "I'm so glad you came, I know you're not into dances, like, who is, ugh, dances, but—"

"Riley, you guys were great." He is so close and smiley and real. I'm emboldened, or crazy. Crazyboldened. I am Making Things Happen.

I lean in and kiss him.

He kisses me back, but he's timid. Whenever you hear about guys and kissing, it's all about how they throw themselves at you and their hands turn into gropey paws, and their tongues turn into bad snake metaphors. The *T* word never comes into play.

"Is this okay?" I ask.

"It's okay," he says, which isn't exactly an I-want-to-do-you-right-now.

"Oh," I say, because it's the best response I can come up with to the response to a question *YOU SHOULD NEVER HAVE TO ASK* upon kissing someone.

He touches my collar, like he's smoothing it down, even though my collar's pretty much impeccable. But it feels like

Ted's making a move—a tiny move, sure, but I'm taking it—and so I lean in for more kissing, which happens, and slightly less timidly at that. My brain is full of thoughts, which is weird because I thought all thoughts would run screaming from my head once my lips made contact with Ted Callahan's. Universe, I am kissing Ted Callahan! Ted Callahan is kissing me! *IN PUBLIC!* Sound the alarms!

Something beeps, which for a second makes me think someone did sound an alarm.

"Oh." Ted takes his phone out of his pocket and checks it. "My mom's here to pick me up."

The thing is, Reid is right about Ted being uncool.

"I can give you a ride," I say.

"Well, she's already here," he says with a smile. "I guess you're going out after this with your band—"

My band! I love that he thinks of us that way.

"—but I'll be up for a while. If you want to email me or something."

"Of course I'll email you." I lean in and kiss him again. "Bye, Ted."

"Bye, Riley."

"Reid!" I shout. He's probably talking to Jane or Jennie or Erika, but I really want to tell him about what just happened.

"Riley!" Reid runs directly at me, like a train off its tracks. We collide and smack foreheads and both fall to the gym floor. I literally see stars. Reid makes dramatic moany sounds.

"What the hell!" I shout into the heavens. The gym's rafters, at least. "Why are the floors so slippery?"

"They just waxed the floor," Reid says. "For basketball preseason."

We continue to lie there, next to each other, somehow both still conscious after the head-smacking and the meet-gym-flooring.

"I have news," I say.

"So do I," Reid says.

"You first!"

"Jane has a boyfriend," Reid says. "He goes to Marshall High, and his mom works for the Society for the Prevention of Cruelty to Animals."

"Crap, Reid, I'm sorry."

We lie there silently for a bit. It's surprisingly not entirely uncomfortable.

"What was your news?" Reid asks.

Of course mere moments ago, when I was still vertical, I was bursting to share everything with Reid. Right now, though, it feels like I'm kicking him while he's—literally—down.

"Want to go get waffles?" I ask instead.

"Ri, I almost always want to go get waffles."

CHAPTER THIRTY-FIVE

Reid's List of Where It Went Wrong

1. Make sure a girl doesn't have a boyfriend.
2. Don't fall in love with someone unless you're sure that person loves you back.

CHAPTER THIRTY-SIX

I make it through waffles with Reid without making his bad night even worse by letting him know that maybe Ted and I are happening. Post-waffle, I let myself into the house without worrying if I'm smiling too much or radiating happy Ted thoughts. Mom and Dad are both up, watching a spy movie, but they hit pause when I come through the door. A secret agent is frozen on-screen, mid-secret.

"How was your show?" Dad asks. "Since we didn't get to see it ourselves."

The United Front had mentioned coming to our show, but this was my night to be a Rock Star in my school. It didn't feel like a rock star move to invite your parents to a school dance.

"Really good. We even got an encore, like a totally legit encore." I sit down with them, even though I'm barely calm enough to sit still. "Someone taped it, so you guys can watch it later, if you want."

"Of course we want," Mom says.

"This is just a general question, like a poll. If someone gets completely rejected, how soon can his friend tell him she finally kissed the guy she super likes?" I ask.

"At least twenty-four hours," Dad says very quickly.

Mom cocks her head at that. "Honesty's an important component of friendship. But if someone's feelings need to be spared, I'm not sure there's a set time limit." The United Front is merely *almost* united for once. "Did something happen tonight—"

"I'm just asking for a friend." I make a face because no one ever believes that. "I should go to bed."

"Okay," the United Front choruses happily.

In my room I approach my computer with proper respect.

There are actually six new emails in my inbox. One is from Nathan, three are just mailing lists from music venues (the Satellite, the Smell, and Bootleg), one is from *MY DAD*, who could just talk to me if he wanted, but the sixth is from exactly who I want it to be.

> to: riley.crowe-ellerman@email.com
> from: ted@edendalefencingclub.com
> subject: Tonight
> Hi Riley,
> Your show was great tonight. Maybe we can hang out this week.
> —Ted

I know it doesn't sound romantic, and I know it's just two sentences plus our names and a *hi*, but I can feel that this is happening. I turn on my best late-night playlist (lots of fuzzy lo-fi and dream pop) and curl up in my pajamas with nothing but thoughts of Ted as I drift off to sleep.

*   *   *

There's a flurry of texts between the Gold Diggers the next morning, which results in the four of us meeting up at Modern Eats for breakfast. I picture us ten years in the future after some amazing gig at the Troubadour.

"Reid, stop it," Lucy says. I'm not really paying attention to the conversation because my brain is full of Ted, but I've heard enough to know that Reid is talking about Jane. Again.

"I'm just saying, if I were her, why would I pick me either?"

"Lots of reasons," Lucy says with hardly any impatience creeping into her tone.

"You could do better," Nathan says, with lots more creeping into his.

"I obviously couldn't!" Reid says.

I know that it's my turn to say something at least vaguely supportive, but my phone beeps, and I grab for it because it could be Ted texting me.

But then I remember that Ted doesn't have my number.

"Who is it?" Reid asks.

I check my phone's screen.

"Milo." I shrug, even though I'm not sure Reid's totally over how I now have a fake ID and he doesn't.

"Cool," Reid says, and he sounds like he means it.

Lucy is looking at me and Reid like she wants to ask who Milo is, but she doesn't.

"I'm working on lining up some more gigs," Nathan says, changing the topic. "I think it's time to make the band our priority, guys."

"It's been my priority," I say, because who the heck says it hasn't been? "It has been for all of us."

"We should book more shows," Nathan says, "and record more demo tracks. Something bigger."

"Nathan's right," Lucy pipes up right away of course.

"We need money for more demo tracks," I say. "It took a while to save up for the three we did record."

"True," Reid says. "But we can pool our money again."

"I used my birthday money last time," I say. "I can't magically have another birthday until April."

"I can cover it," Nathan says, and we all stare at him because that's weird. Even Lucy is giving him a *WTF?* look. Yes, we all know Nathan lives in a big house in Franklin Hills, but it's truly never been some kind of dividing line before. "What? I can. It's no big deal."

"We know you can," I say.

"I just save my money." Nathan shrugs like he's just better at allowance than we are and not that his parents don't have their own TV production company. "It's not a big deal. It'll be good to cut more demo tracks, maybe find a way to do a whole EP."

It's not that anything Nathan's doing is bad, but this has always been about the four of us, and I don't like it that he seems to be taking control just because he has more money than we do.

"Let's think about it," Lucy says. "Focus on more shows for now, maybe?"

"Yeah," Reid says, and I'm glad no one apparently wants to take Nathan's money and run. "More gigs would be good."

"Okay." It's clear from his deep sigh, Nathan knows he's defeated. "We do need to think about recording more, though."

"We know," Lucy says in her sweet but teasing tone, and I can't help but grin at her because, duh, Nathan, we get it.

Afterward I can tell Reid is hoping we'll all hang out longer, dissecting all the ways the Jane situation sucks, but we all have or are pretending to have plans that don't allow for more of that. My plans are literally going home to email Ted, but I still don't quite know how to present this information to Reid without crushing him even more.

So I just say nothing. And at home I respond to Ted's email from last night. I also finally respond to Milo, and we make plans to hang out on Sunday. Even after the dance, I'm not certain Ted's a sure thing yet, and there's no reason not to see Milo in the meantime.

CHAPTER THIRTY-SEVEN

Ways Milo Is Amazing, by Riley (OBVIOUSLY)

1. Has fake ID and the ability to get more fake IDs!
2. Has the confidence to pull off the tuba.
3. Apparently has some kind of magical ability to always know about upcoming shows, even ones that aren't publicized.
4. Says his favorite shake at the Oinkster is the ube, so he has good taste and isn't afraid of unique flavors/colors.
5. Acts really casual but never like he's too good for stuff.
6. Is gorgeous like guys you see in black-and-white photos about CBGB's heyday.
7. Despite #6, is clearly into ME.

CHAPTER THIRTY-EIGHT

I take my sweet frigging time getting ready Monday morning because as much as I want to see Ted—who finally responded to my email but with nothing concrete or specific about the hanging out we're going to do this week—I still want to appear casual. I will not seem like the girl stalking her own inbox or replaying the fall formal's kisses in her head as if they're the winning touchdown after the Super Bowl.

But after dropping Ashley off at the middle school, I can't avoid Edendale, since I don't feel like another late slip, so I head over and park. A guy I barely know stares me down as I walk through the parking lot, and I have no idea what this is about, but it is not putting me in a *casual* mood.

"You were so awesome at the dance," he says.

Oh!

"Thanks," I say. It is the first of *SIX TIMES* I get to thank someone for a similar or even identical compliment just on my way to my locker. There's even a random present from some anonymous worshipper in my locker! Someone shoved in a mix CD, somehow, and labeled in pretty great penmanship is a good array of songs from bands that all have kick-ass drummers, including Superchunk, Lightning Bolt, Flaming Lips, Wild Flag, the Descendants, and the Minutemen, and even some old-school stuff like the Who and the Velvet Underground. I love CDs, and I love gifts so, thank you, anonymous person. You're awesome.

I don't find Ted, but at least I can't seem too forceful if I'm not all up in his face. The kissing might not even mean huge new perfect things! I kissed Garrick and Milo and nothing huge or new or perfect is going on with them. Sometimes kissing is just kissing, and I don't want to get ahead of myself.

Especially with Ted.

"Riley," Garrick greets me when I walk into chemistry. "I heard you guys were awesome. I'm sorry I couldn't go."

"We should have a video we'll put up on our site soon," I say.

"Also this week is less crazy if you want to hang out or something."

"Sure," I say, but then I think about Ted. "Though... maybe just to study."

Garrick shoves his hair all around. "Did you hear something? About you-know-who?"

"Voldemort?" Why did I ask that? Riley, get it together. "Sorry, that's stupid, just, no, what?"

He leans over and scribbles on my worksheet. *I hung out with Sydney this weekend.*

My brain is spinning. Okay, I was literally probably just about to stop whatever has been happening with Garrick, and now maybe that's been taken care of for me. But is Garrick with Sydney again? When he could have me? Except, wait, no, things might really be happening with Ted. And of course there's Milo who is so straightforward and uncomplicated and what you'd find in the dictionary under *rock*, if dictionaries used photos of cute guys to make points.

Mr. Landiss starts talking, so I pick up my pen. *It's okay. We weren't official at all!*

Garrick nods and leans over again. *It just kind of happened, and I didn't want you to hear from someone else. I was going to tell you in person and not at school if I could help it. I'm sorry. You're great.*

It's OK! I write. *WE ARE FINE! You are great too!* ☺

I think about telling him I was just about to end things anyway, but Mr. Landiss starts yammering about Bunsen burners, and of course Garrick's taking attentive notes. And I decide things really *are* fine, and flash back to Friday night some more instead.

* * *

After school Ted's at *my* locker for once.

"Hi, Riley," he says.

"Hey, what are you doing now? After school, I mean. Are you busy?" I ask, then worry I'm being too eager after I was also the one to kiss him first. I've held off all day from acting too eager. "I mean, no big deal if you are, or if you aren't but you have something else to do."

Ted smiles like my babbling isn't annoying. "Actually I have to intern at my mom's office tonight."

"Do you need a ride? I can take you."

"I was going to say, I can be a few minutes late. So, a ride would be great, and we can maybe hang out for a while."

I wonder if we're going to spend those few minutes making out, but instead we end up at Silverlake Coffee. Ted's quiet like he normally is, and it's easy to believe I didn't actually kiss him on Friday night. It's even easier to believe he didn't kiss me back. But when we get back into my car with our cranberry chais—which don't really taste like cranberry or chai but are yummy regardless—I lean over a little and we're kissing again. I know it's not fair to compare, but when I'd kissed Garrick, it was like those kisses were Going Somewhere. But when Ted and I are kissing, it's like the destination doesn't even matter because every single moment seems like it couldn't get better.

"I guess we should probably go," he says during a pause. "I'm sorry. My mom got this whole internship set up for me to help with my college applications next year, and I don't want to flake on it."

"Your mom sounds really cool," I say for some reason. After that I stay pretty quiet as we drive over to the office.

"Thanks for the ride, Riley," he says, and then he's gone.

I shove the secret admirer's CD into my stereo. My phone

rings, but it's no secret admirer getting less secret. It's just Reid.

"Yo," I say, mainly to taunt him.

"Riley, I don't care what you're doing, you have to come over here now."

"I was actually—"

"It doesn't matter what! This is an *emergency.*"

"Are you dying?" I ask. Probably not if he's on the phone with me, but I still feel like I should check.

"My soul is dying," he says very seriously.

I'm not that worried about him because this is the second time this school year he's said his soul was dying. But I still drive over to his house. I'm in the process of parking when I know what's up because Reid is standing in front of his house holding a leash that is attached to the cutest black fluffy dog.

"Oh my god!" I leap out of the car as it's still settling in place alongside the curb. "You got a dog!"

"No, Riley, I did not *get* a dog," Reid says. "I was *dogged.*"

"That's not a thing." I jump back and forth in front of the dog so it'll join in, and it does. Nothing in life is wrong when you are bouncing around with canine friends. "This is the best dog. You're so lucky; my parents say we can't have pets because 'we're both too busy to help.'"

"Riley, I don't *want* this dog," Reid says. "When I got home, Mom was there and acting all weird, and then the doorbell rings and it's Jane's boss from Paws for People with this dog."

"The dog you pretended you were going to adopt so you

could win Jane over," I say, scratching the dog between its ears. "Oh my god, what are you going to name it? Is it a boy or a girl?"

"It's a boy." Reid shakes his head. "I had this whole plan of going back and saying I didn't know my brother had allergies—"

"Michael's allergic to dogs?" I ask. Reid's older brother, who is crazy good-looking in a frat-boy manner and off in Chicago at Northwestern, hasn't spent enough significant time around me for me to be knowledgeable about his allergies.

"No, Riley, that was just the plan to bail on the dog. But I forgot about the plan, since it seemed like I was getting somewhere with Jane—"

"It did," I say. "It wasn't you being crazy. It was—"

"Anyway," Reid says, cutting me off. "So the last time we talked about the dog, I said I didn't know if my mom would be okay with it or not because she'd probably rather I get a purebred dog from a breeder instead of a rescue."

"She must have gotten all riled up," I say, because Jane is on this one-girl mission to educate people at Edendale about the thirteen bajillion reasons it's better to rescue a pet. She has brochures stuck to her locker and a handwritten sign that says, TAKE ONE, PLEASE!! ☺

"Yes, she did, and thinking she was being *nice* to me, she called my mom and explained it all to her."

"Wait, you made up an allergy for Michael, but you gave your mom's real number?"

166

"She could have checked that! She couldn't check if Michael was allergic. And I was *going to* make up his allergy. I didn't even get a chance."

I sit down on the ground so it's easier to pet the dog. This dog has immediately become at least my third best friend in ranking. "Seriously, what are you going to name him? He needs the best, fluffiest name."

I think about telling Reid about my list of kitten names but as awesome as this dog is, I'm not going to sacrifice one of my names.

"Riley, this is a disaster! Why aren't you acting like it's a disaster?"

"It's not a disaster." I know Reid wants me to share his devastation but I just can't. "Jane was actually trying to do something nice for you, and so was your mom. You should feel special. And now you have a dog. A dog! You're so lucky."

Reid plunks down next to me on the ground. "I guess I'm going to name him Peabody. You know, like Rocky and Bullwinkle's genius dog."

I don't know, because unlike Reid, I'm not a weirdo about old cartoons, but I don't want to discourage him. "That's a great name." I pat his shoulder. "See? This is great."

He doesn't agree out loud, but I think maybe he does agree. Or at least somewhere deep down inside his weird Reid heart.

"You have to get him a cool collar," I say. "That one's supergeneric."

"Yeah, I know," he says with a sigh like he's carrying the entire world's problems on his shoulders.

"We could walk over to that pet store on Hillhurst," I say, nodding in its general direction.

"Sure." He perks up as we're walking over. "Girls like dogs, right? Like maybe I'll get attention from girls if I'm walking Peabody?"

"Maybe," I say, "sure."

"Are you going to the Andrew Mothereffing Jackson show at the Satellite on Thursday?" I ask.

"Maybe," he says. "If I can find a girl to go with me—which I think I can."

CHAPTER THIRTY-NINE

Girls Who Might Go Out with Me, Post-Fall Formal, by Reid

1. Erika Ennis--all but said she'd go out with me, so she's a sure bet.
2. Jennie Leung--hasn't said anything per se, but she's as sure of a bet without actually being a sure bet as someone could be.
3. Madison Price--said "we should hang out sometime, Reid," so I'm as good as in there.
4. Sierra Myers--told me I looked cool onstage--as good as in!
5. Diana Ruiz--found random excuses to talk to me in the hallway and in the cafeteria, which she's never done before. As good as in!

6. Katelyn Foster--see number five.
7. Brianna Bennett--see number five.
8. Natalie Garcia--see number five.
9. Sophie Chang--see number five.
10. Michelle Howard--was just kind of staring at me a lot during sociology and Western civ, but when I sort of caught her and made eye contact, finally she smiled at me. As good as in.

CHAPTER FORTY

I'm early for our next practice, which is on Wednesday night this week only to accommodate the Andrew Mothereffing Jackson show. In the old days, I showed up early all the time, so I hope Lucy won't make anything significant of it. I'm relieved when she just lets me inside the house and asks if I want snacks. Who doesn't want snacks!

"I told Reid to bring his dog to practice, but I don't know if he's going to," she says. "I really want to meet him, though."

"He's an awesome dog," I say. "You'll love him. I wish I could have a dog."

"Me too," she says. "I'd love that."

"At least you have a cat! The United Front is totally anti-pet, period."

My phone beeps, and I dig it out of my purse to check it. It's from Milo, and it's awesome. secret coyote dreams show tonight @ echoplex - b there? I text back immediately because the newest Coyote Dreams album is seriously awesome. when??? i have practice but could come after!!!!

Lucy watches me text but doesn't say anything.

My phone beeps again. 9 - can u make it? I can, so I respond in a happy affirmative manner and shove the phone back into my bag. Reid arrives—sans Peabody—and I point toward the garage, even though Nathan's not here yet. "Should we go get started?"

"We should wait for Nathan," Lucy says, of course. "You guys are both going to the Andrew Mothereffing Jackson show tomorrow, right?"

"Yep," Reid says with a nod and a smile. "I am, at least. With Madison Price."

"Really, Madison Price?" Lucy asks, as I accidentally say "Ew, no" aloud. But ew, no. Madison Price is seriously the worst type of person. Well, not compared to murderers and rapists and tax evaders or whatever, but besides that, *yes*. She dresses like she only shops in the little boutiques on Sunset in Silver Lake and Echo Park, like an American Apparel explosion, and she wears this stupid feather earring all the time. I guess in truth she looks cool, but what I hate about her is that she constantly walks around with this bored expression like she's too good for life. Listen, Madison, no one's too good for life. We're all living it; get over yourself.

"Why 'really'?" Reid asks Lucy. "Does it seem like I couldn't go out with her? Do you think everyone's going to think that?"

"Reid, that isn't what I mean," she says as Nathan walks in. "She's just so—"

"*HORRIBLE!*" I say—again, accidentally. "Her face is the worst."

"Who?" Nathan helps himself to a soda from the refrigerator.

Wait, he lets himself in *AND* gets his own beverages? Is this what happens when someone has sex with you?

"Madison Price," Reid says.

"Oh, right," Nathan says, and makes the *bored* face. Lucy and I both lose it. "She's actually not that bad."

"Guys, I know, but..." Reid looks defeated. "She's—"

"Really hot," I fill in, because what else is she? Popular. Okay. "Can we please start? I have a lot I need to do tonight."

"I bet you do," Reid says.

"I bet you do," I chipmunk back.

Then we both laugh, and we head to the garage to practice. Since "Tease," "Garage," and "Incandescent" are pretty polished by this point, we spend a lot of time on "Riverside Drive," "Screwed Up Again," and a few covers. It's an easy practice, and I am ready to get on with my night, but I should have known a certain topic had not been shut down forever.

"Have you guys thought any more about cutting an EP?" Nathan asks as he gently packs his Rickenbacker in its case.

"Nope," I say, attempting to set a new speed record for packing up my drums. "Remember, no money."

"Severe no money," Lucy says.

"Eh, less severe no money," Reid says. "But still no money."

I head to the door. "See you guys tomorrow."

"Riley, hang on," Nathan says. "Can we seriously discuss this?"

"I thought we *were* seriously discussing it," Lucy says with a smile. "I want to focus on getting better and writing more songs."

"And getting seen," Reid says. "We get seen by enough people, we won't have to finance something on our own."

"Guys, I have to go." My voice comes out sounding like Ashley whining to stay up late so she can *NON-IRONICALLY* watch another episode of *Toddlers and Tiaras*. "Sorry, I just have plans."

Reid walks me out. "Garrick?"

"Milo. Secret show at the Echoplex. Coyote Dreams."

"Nice," Reid says.

I start to tell Reid that I've ended things with Garrick, but I haven't brought up Ted yet. And at this point I know I should, but it feels like a longer conversation than I have time for right now, and I don't feel like getting the inevitable dozen follow-up texts while I'm seeing Coyote Dreams. So I just say good-bye and go.

Milo has already staked out a prime spot in line when I arrive, which is great because every single show at the Echoplex ends up with a line snaked down the block. He gives me a tight hug when I walk up. "You made it. How was practice?"

"Semi-good, semi-annoying. So, the usual."

"Yeah, I'm pretty sure that's how every Arcade Fire practice goes."

"Nathan wants us to record an EP, which would be great, except that it costs money we obviously don't have."

Milo nods.

"Except Nathan actually has all this money because his parents are rich, so he's all, oh, I'll just pay for it, no big deal," I say. "But it's like if we let him just do that—"

"He has the power in the band," Milo finishes for me.

"Exactly! And that would be bad enough, but Nathan's practically a dictator as it is. He's so bossy about *everything* and is always, like, hey guys, let's be really serious about things, the way I am."

It's possible I'm making Nathan sound even assier than he actually is, but I'm comfortable with it because it still feels like I'm conveying the truth.

"I could beat that guy up for you," Milo says, and I think he's kidding, but I also think he actually *could.* I devote a moment or five to imagining that beatdown.

Milo nudges me, but in a suave not-trying-too-hard way. "What are you smiling about?"

I don't think Milo should know I'm fantasizing about his beautiful fists landing on Nathan's—fine, also beautiful face. "Oh, uh, something unrelated, completely. So you're going to the Andrew Mothereffing Jackson show tomorrow, right?"

"Tomorrow's actually a game day," he says. "I'll be marching my magnificent beast of a tuba across the field in South Pasadena. But you can come watch if you want."

I make a face without meaning to, but luckily Milo laughs right away.

"Trust me, no sane person would have taken me up on that offer," he says. "But it was fun seeing just how horrified that made you."

"Not because of your tuba," I say. "I'm sure it's super-magnificent, like you say. Just—they're one of my favorite bands. I can't miss them."

"And I wouldn't want you to." Milo grins at me. "Especially for my tuba."

* * *

Ted's waiting at my locker the next morning. "Hi, Riley."

He's wearing a *Dinosaur Comics* shirt, which honestly makes me a little weak. Cool T-shirts work a number on me like fancy cologne probably does on other girls.

"Hey," I say.

"I don't have to intern tonight," he says. "Or work."

I wait for what feels like the obvious asking-out that's going to occur. But it's just a long pause. Ted! We have kissed! We have kissed on two separate occasions! Why aren't we at the witty-banter stage yet, Ted?

"So do you want to hang out?" I ask.

"Yes," Ted says as a smile takes over his face. Maybe Ted's just as unsure as I am? "Meet me at my locker at the end of the day?"

"I'll be there with bells on," I say for some reason, even though I normally steer way clear of old-timey phrases. Ted! Why do you bring out the dorkiest in me?

"You don't have to go that far," he says, still smiling, and waves before heading off down the hallway.

Later at lunch, while Lucy and Nathan are having an intense discussion about whether or not the Dunlop Cry Baby guitar pedal is overrated, I turn to Reid.

"So... things ended with Garrick," I say.

"Really?" he asks. "Why?"

"Garrick's in love with Sydney again. And also... I kissed Ted."

"Just now?" Reid looks around like maybe Ted's under the table.

"Friday night. After our set." I take a long sip of water to buy me a moment. "And Monday, too. Like, things are happening."

"Okay," Reid says. "Why didn't you tell me sooner?"

"Just because of... stuff with... Jane? I didn't want to make you feel worse."

"So, wait, you thought I couldn't handle hearing about it? That I have to be *protected*?"

Reid's volume goes up enough that even the Dunlop Cry Baby can't keep Lucy and Nathan from looking over.

"No, not *protected*. I was just trying to be nice," I say.

"I don't need you to be nice, Ri," he says, and I don't argue that, even though I feel like Reid needs that more than he needs a lot of things.

"Do you want some pretzels, Reid?" Lucy holds out a little bag of Rold Gold to him.

"No, I don't want pretzels, and I don't want to be protected, and I don't want you to be nice. I'm doing great!"

Lucy and I exchange *whoa-he's-deluded* looks. And I take some pretzels if Reid isn't going to.

"I'm going to talk to Madison," he says, and gathers all his stuff. He has notebooks and textbooks and a Craig Thompson graphic novel and his iPod out on the table, so the gathering is a pretty extended activity. We all watch like it's a spectator sport.

After school, I meet Ted by his locker. Reid's still avoiding me, and that's fine. I mean, it's not *great*, but I don't have time to dwell on specifically where it falls on the annoyance scale. I am hanging out with Ted Callahan!

"Where do you want to go?" I ask Ted.

"Wherever." He shrugs as he gets books off of the little blue plastic shelf in his locker. It doesn't come across with any particular enthusiasm, but I decide that's just Ted.

"Fred Sixty-Two?" I ask because it's my default, and so I can get a waffle. Ted agrees, and we're off. Rain has begun dripping down from the gray sky, and parking is terrible. But Ted has an umbrella with him (!!!) to shelter us. We have to walk close together to use it, and we bump into each other a few times. Unfortunately, nothing sexy like hand-holding happens.

I grab a booth in the back and pretend to browse the menu

because maybe Ted won't think it's hot that I'm a girl so sure of waffles. Ted's very intent on his menu, so when he closes it, I'm hopeful we're going to have some amazing conversation. But Ted is so just... Ted. Despite that we have had Real Significant Moments, he's quietly glancing down at his place mat and then checking his phone and then all attention back on the place mat once again.

"I like your shirt," I say because it's too quiet but also because I do.

Ted smiles before he even looks up. "Thanks. I like yours, too."

I'm not even wearing a cool T-shirt, so it feels like an extra-nice compliment.

A waiter takes our orders, and even though Ted orders a perfectly reasonable club sandwich, he does not raise his eyebrows at my waffle order. It's definitely a quality I need in a guy: nonjudgmental of waffles. Also, obviously, good hair and good taste in music. Ted is perfect. Ted, you're perfect! I am a hopeless case of love. Wait, love? Am I really thinking this is love? It's Something, and maybe turning into Something More, but love is probably getting ahead of myself.

"Did you do anything last weekend?" I ask Ted, who is drawing a sketch of a robot on his place mat instead of making scintillating conversation with me.

"I worked and helped my mom run some errands." He adds antennae to the robot's head. "And did homework. Pretty boring. What about you? See ten secret shows?"

"I wish! Mainly just band stuff. We're trying to work really hardcore to focus on getting as strong as possible."

He's still drawing. "Well, you're in really good shape already."

There is no way to pack in how much I love him saying that into one word, but I try anyway. "Thanks."

Ted adds some text to the robot (I HATE MAGNETS!), and I stare at the words for a few moments. I have seen this handwriting before.

"You made me that mix CD." It flies out of my mouth like an accusation, so I try to soften my tone. "I mean, you did. Did you?"

Ted looks confused. "The one I gave you on Monday, you mean?"

I'm back to thinking maybe Ted has the best taste in music of anyone I know. Would it be weird to ask him to the Andrew Mothereffing Jackson show tonight? Is that Too Much Riley at Once? "Yeah. Someone left me this awesome CD, and I had no idea who."

"I put a note on it!" he says. "It wasn't supposed to be anonymous."

"The note said, 'To Riley'! That's still anonymous!"

Ted laughs. "I meant to sign it. I didn't intend any mystery."

"Good, because I solved it pretty quickly."

"I just wanted to do something nice for you," he says.

"Thanks," I say. "It's a really good CD."

"I did a lot of research," he says. "On bands that have good drummers. And I checked with my cousin, and he helped me, too."

Okay, so Ted is no musical genius. Ted's mix CD required the Internet and his cousin. But that probably took even more effort than if he'd just had perfect taste, and he used all that effort on *me*. I feel like crawling under the table and joining him on his side of the booth for a big hug and some cuddling and the sharing of our forthcoming food.

I manage to stay put, though. Despite how it feels to have someone good and pure and of course completely hot like Ted do something like that for me.

I haven't written anything about Ted in the Passenger Manifest. I know I'm not *required* to, but it was easy with Garrick, and it's been easy with Milo. And it's not at all about hurting or not hurting Reid's feelings. It's that right now, Ted is just for me.

CHAPTER FORTY-ONE

<u>The Madison Thing, by Reid</u>

Madison Price was one of the first people to say something nice to me after the fall formal. So it seemed like I had an in with her, and then she asked me if I was going to the Andrew Mothereffing Jackson show. She just asked me like it was a normal thing we talk about, and not like up until then we never spoke at all. (Well, a couple times in geometry last year she had to borrow paper from me, but it didn't ever seem like it could progress past that.)

So I waited for a good moment (she walked up to me in the hallway and said hi and actually stopped, didn't just keep walking like someone who's not interested would probably do) and straight-out asked

her if she wanted to go with me. After
everything that happened with Jane I'm
not going to get all mixed up in something
weird and hopeless again.

Luckily and amazingly, Madison said yes!
She gave me her phone number and email
address and said we should hang out first. I
didn't want to seem desperate or weirdly eager
so I waited a day to call her, and when she
answered she said, "Reid, FI-nally."

We didn't actually talk for very long but she
said she'd see me tomorrow, like it's a special
thing instead of us just seeing each other at
school like we always do, and for a minute—
well, more than a minute—I worried it might
be some weird prank, but the next morning she
was hanging near my locker and then talked
to me until we had to get to class.

I kinda figured when I had my pick of girls
after the dance I would ask out Erika or Jennie,
but Madison just made it really easy, and I never
really thought I could get anyone as popular
as she is, so if I'd known, maybe I would have
put her in my top three anyway. And now I'm not
going to fall in love with a girl only to have my
heart pulverized, so this is a great solution.

184

CHAPTER FORTY-TWO

Since Milo can't set aside his tuba, and since I'm not sure if Ted and I are at Seeing Each Other Multiple Times on the Same Day level yet, I have no guy to accompany me to the Andrew Mothereffing Jackson show. I used to go to shows all the time without guys—Reid doesn't count—but tonight is another story. Because I'm now at the Satellite with LucyAndNathan and ReidAndMadison.

I am the Fifth Wheel Legend, always in the way.

Lesser people would have canceled. But I do not miss shows. For reasons other than being stuck in Colonial Williamsburg, at least.

"This is nice, right?" Reid asks me while we're checking out the merch table. Lucy and Nathan are securing our spot, and Madison's in the bathroom probably putting on lip gloss or eyeliner or whatever—her makeup always looks perfect. I guess having a date means Reid's over having his feelings hurt. That's maybe the one positive outcome from this Madison development.

"The Satellite? Sure, we haven't been here in a while," I say, even though I know that's not what he means.

"Madison's cool," he says as if that will convince me. "And it's cool being out with Lucy and Nathan, doing couple stuff."

"That's the lamest thing I've ever heard you say, which is saying something." I know I'm being a jerk, but I don't care. I know if he was the only one without a date we'd all have to comfort him. "Why can't you go out with someone nice you actually like?"

"I like her." Reid examines a T-shirt. "What do you think?"

"It's definitely the coolest one." I'm glad Lucy and I have maintained control of Reid's wardrobe, and it hasn't gone back to his mom.

Reid gets cash out of his pocket to buy the shirt. "Do you really not like her?"

This much concertgoing should have already taught Reid that the smartest time to buy any merch is on your way out so you don't have to clutch some obnoxious thing all night long while you're trying to just listen and have a great time. But I let him buy it, and he doesn't seem to notice I never answer his question.

He heads back over to Madison and therefore Lucy and Nathan, but I hang back. After only a moment of deliberation I get my—or I should say Jennifer Anne Matthews's—ID out of my purse and buy a beer. The beer-buying versus beer-receiving part of my life is new, so I just pick the first kind— Stella—on the list. Good news! It tastes like a beer.

The opener, Remington Steele, comes out, and I shove my way to the front so I'm near our group plus Madison. Lucy looks to my beer and raises an eyebrow, but it's too loud to explain and even if it wasn't I wouldn't. Remington Steele's set is loud and fun and fast and I'm not sure I could ever be in a bad mood at a show once it's actually happening so I just grin at her.

Once the set is over I dash off to the bathroom. One beer apparently does the work of many sodas on my bladder. On my way back out, I think about getting a soda because while beer is the coolest of concert beverages, I actually like root beer better.

And then I'm sure I start hallucinating because this thing I see cannot be a thing that's happening right now. Does one lousy beer make you hallucinate?

"Hi, Riley." Ted waves from a distance, and then suddenly he's close. Oh, wait, he just walked over quickly. That part isn't weird. "I was wondering if you'd be here."

"Of course I'm here," I say, and grin at him. Because I wish one of us would have just asked the other one. But you wondered, Ted, you wondered!

"I knew they were one of your favorite bands," he says, which is a fair guess given my multiple T-shirts and the button on my bag. "So I thought I'd check them out. I would have gotten here for the opening band, but I had to close at work."

A rush of relief hits me that Milo's busy with his tuba. I'd thought juggling was fine if your juggled items went to two different schools. "You'll love them," I say. "Where do you work anyway?"

"I, uh, I don't really want to say." Ted laughs. "I have to wear a pretty stupid hat."

"Oh my god, now you have to tell me," I say.

"It's bad," he says. "It was just the first place that was hiring when I went into the mall, and my mom said I had to get a job."

I poke at his shoulder. "You have to tell me."

"No, I'd have to yell it here, and I'm not yelling it." Ted grins at me.

We get sodas, and I—*AGAINST ALL MY BETTER JUDGMENT*—lead Ted over to the spot the group's got staked out. Everyone just greets him enthusiastically—well, except Madison, who gives him an expression-free nod. Lucy gives me the same look she gave me over the beer. Grinning back seemed to work before, so I do it again.

When Andrew Mothereffing Jackson's crazy drummer counts off for the first song, I feel that switch flip in me. It's so good to be standing here in this crowd—Madison included—even though she's making an obviously forced bored expression and only vaguely nodding to the beat. The rest of us are jumping around and singing along, and it's the best thing in the world how every good show becomes the best night you've ever had.

* * *

Ted is planning on taking the bus home afterward, so after bypassing pizza because it's way too late to be out for even those of us with very lenient parents, I offer to give him a ride.

188

"I'll tell you, if you don't tell anyone else," Ted says as I'm making a U-turn on Silver Lake Boulevard I'm pretty sure is legal.

I have no idea what he's talking about, but I'm going to have a secret with Ted!

"Hot Dog on a Stick."

"What?" I pull up to a stoplight and look over at him. "Wait, do you work at Hot Dog on a Stick?"

"You can't tell anyone," he says really fast.

"Oh my god!" Hot Dog on a Stick is this fast-food place in the food court that sells corn dogs and fried cheese—on a stick, of course, and deliciously tart lemonade. Also their uniforms are *ridiculous*. "Do you have to wear a striped fez?"

"No! Those are for girls! I just have to wear a baseball hat."

I try not to laugh, but it happens anyway. "I'm sorry. Do you at least get free hot dogs?"

"Yeah, I get free hot dogs."

"Do you have to wear those short-shorts?"

"No, those are also just for girls. My shorts are normal length."

"But you wear shorts!" I've never seen Ted in shorts. My mind goes electrical imagining it. "Can I come in and see you work?"

He grins some more at me. "I can't stop you."

I am in love with grinning now. Also maybe Ted. No, Riley! Stop thinking about love!

"That was a great show," I say. "Did you like it?"

I hold my breath because if he didn't, where will that lead us, Ted, where?

"Yeah," Ted says. "They were great. I looked it up, and actually they were at FYF Fest last year, too, while you were looking at wigs."

"Colonial Williamsburg ruins everything," I say, which makes him laugh.

"Thanks for the ride," he says as I'm pulling up to his apartment complex. "See you tomorrow, Riley."

I don't have the right words, but I reach for his hand as he unbuckles his seat belt, and that must be good enough because he leans in and kisses me.

"Good night," I tell him, obviously with my hands in his amazing hair.

"Good night, Riley."

I wave as he gets out of my car. He glances back at me and waves again. And I suddenly don't think I'm overreacting to think maybe it's not yet but is turning into love.

CHAPTER FORTY-THREE

The Madison Thing, Continued, by Reid

After the Andrew Mothereffing Jackson
show, I figure we'll have to go home because
everyone else says they have to, but once
we're in my car, Madison asks if I have a
curfew. I don't, but even if I did I would
lie right now. I don't think curfews seem
especially manly.

So we discuss what's still open, which
is a list I've carefully cultivated, but
Madison comes up with ideas I didn't
even know about. We end up just driving to
that big fountain near the park by the S.
I figured late at night there's probably
drug dealers or prostitutes hanging around
but actually it's really safe, just people
walking dogs.

191

We walk around and it hits me this is a really romantic place. So even though I prefer situations where you're around 95 percent guaranteed to have a kiss welcomed (like, a girl says "kiss me" or at least you're playing Seven Minutes in Heaven), I just go for it, and unbelievably Madison kisses me back.

It's the best kiss of my life. We keep kissing, and Madison puts her arms around me like we've done this a million times. I go for her hair with my hands and then her face and then her back, like, in the safe back zone, not too close to her butt or anything, and we're still kissing and it's great.

I'm starting to think I might actually get away with touching her butt when there's a siren and flashing lights, and I knew I was right that there are probably dealers or hookers here or something. But Madison starts laughing, and I realize the cops are coming up to us.

They ask how old we are, and Madison says she doesn't know, which is funny but, holy crap, she shouldn't be joking around with cops. Luckily, they laugh and tell us to go home, that it's too late for us to be out. So we run to the car, and Madison says we should go get pie at House of Pies, and even if my mom wasn't always warning me about the health code problems that place is always having, I'd say we should go home because, shit, the cops!

Madison doesn't act like I'm being a nerd, so that's good. She asks me who the last person I kissed was, so I tell her because it was that girl at my cousin's birthday party which isn't an embarrassing story, and she tells me for her it was Garrick Bell and I don't say anything about Riley even when Madison says Garrick is "surprisingly good at stuff" which could be a direct quote from Riley. I just laugh and act like I'm cool with hearing her talk about kissing other guys, which I'm really not.

I take her home and we spend thirteen more minutes kissing before she gets out of the car. (I check the car's clock.) It was a perfect night, but I'm sure by tomorrow she'll have completely changed her mind.

CHAPTER FORTY-FOUR

Reid walks up alongside me as I'm on my way to chemistry the next day.

"Yo."

"Stop that," I say.

"Last night was fun," he says. "Ted's actually pretty cool."

"I told you so."

"So have you ended things with Milo—"

"Don't say his name," I say. "Someone could hear you."

"You mean *Ted* could hear me."

"Don't say his name, either!"

"Riley," he says. "What are you doing?"

"I'm not exclusive with anyone. I'm free and clear and an independent woman!"

"No, Riley. This isn't about your independence, which, yes, you have in abundance."

In abundance?

"What I'm saying is, remember what happened with Jane and me?"

"This is different." I am positive it is. Jane has a *boyfriend.* Milo isn't my boyfriend, and neither is Ted.

"How?" he asks. "Aren't you leading them both on?"

I glare at him because he isn't not making sense. Okay, I'm pretty sure I'm not *leading anyone on.* But also I know I am having Big Important feelings for Ted, and yet I still sent Milo a text about the show.

"I'm not, and everything's fine," I say, because we've reached my classroom and also because I am way the heck over this conversation. "See you later."

* * *

After dinner that night with Mom and Dad and Ashley, I check my phone to find a multitude of text messages. Milo is just saying *hey* because that's how he rolls, casual but thoughtful. Garrick wants to make sure I'll check my email later because he sent me an "interesting science journal article." Okay, Garrick, we'll see about that. Reid has also texted, which is nothing exciting, just telling me he thinks the new Waxahatchee album is great—which it is, but I'm not feeling great about anything to do with Reid, so, whatever, I do not respond.

I'm sad to realize there's no message from Ted. Ted doesn't even have my phone number, but he's smart. Ted, you're smart! You can get it somehow. You can, and once you've procured my digits, reach out to me and say something clever that warms my heart and makes me laugh like there's a wonderful private joke between us.

I realize if I talked this out with someone, I might be able to get good, solid advice. But there is no acceptable advice-giver in my whole life right now. Reid will probably just lecture me about dating multiple guys, Lucy and I are not that kind of friends anymore, and Nathan has never been that kind of friend to begin with.

It seriously sucks to feel super alone, even with a phone full of messages.

I think of something, and sit down at my computer and type without thinking. Sure, it's a Friday night, and sure, we've seen each other a lot this week. But I just do it!

> to: ted@edendalefencingclub.com
> from: riley.crowe-ellerman@email.com
> subject: hey
> hi ted,
> last night was fun. are you up to something awesome tonight? or are you deep-frying hot dogs?
> —riley

I know it's kind of lame, but he responds almost immediately, like magic I conjured up.

> to: riley.crowe-ellerman@email.com

from: ted@edendalefencingclub.com

subject: RE: hey

No, I can't deep-fry anything because I'm not at work.
I'm up to doing homework, which probably isn't what
you have in mind by "something awesome."

to: ted@edendalefencingclub.com

from: riley.crowe-ellerman@email.com

subject: RE: hey

you should call me, it's easier than email! 323-555-3764

The second I click on send I leap away from my computer
and my phone and I pace the circumference of my room like
it's a geometry theorem I have to prove with my feet.

But then my phone rings.

"Hello?" I say in my best casual voice.

"Hi, Riley," Ted says.

"Hi," I say.

We're waiting-for-a-funeral-to-start silent. Without the
tears.

"Are you busy?" I ask.

"I called you," he says.

"I know, but I told you to!"

"Not at gunpoint or anything."

"I think you knew if you didn't call I would shoot you," I
say, which I'm not sure is funny or supercreepy. "I mean, I
know where you live."

Okay, that was not even debatable; it was just flat-out creepy. Ted, I'm sorry! Ted, I'd never stalk you and shoot you; that's the weirdest.

Luckily he laughs. "Yeah, I knew all of that. It's why I called. I was terrified."

"Do you want to go to the Nadia + Friends show tomorrow night?" I'm sure he's never heard of them, but he's actually a great concertgoer, and not just because of the kissing after.

"I can't. I have work," he says. "I guess you're going."

"I'm not sure yet," I say. "My parents let me go out a lot this week so I might have run out of super-late nights."

"Yeah, my mom gets like that, too," Ted says. "I get it, but it's annoying."

My phone beeps, and I pull it back from my ear to see who's calling. It's Reid, almost like he knows. I very firmly with tons of conviction press ignore, as though Reid could feel the snub through his phone line. I picture him feeling it and reacting in a big, over-the-top manner, and it's awesome. Wait, no, it isn't awesome. What a jerk thing to think.

"How's your world history homework going?" he asks.

"I'm going to do it soon," I say. "You're probably finished already."

Wait, did that sound like an insult? It isn't an insult. He's just so responsible! Who knew that quality could be so dreamy on a guy? (Not me.)

"Yeah, I don't think it's too great, but I finished it. You'll probably be more creative with yours."

I had no idea guys could make you feel swoony with talk of homework.

"I guess I should let you go," he says. "You have homework, and I'm probably going to watch *Blind Love.*"

"Oh my god! That show's my *favorite.* It's so amazingly bad."

"I know," he says with sexy conviction. Well, it probably isn't supposed to sound sexy, but I like strong emotions from Ted. Ted, we've come so far from that first day in my car! "See you soon, Riley."

* * *

I spend Saturday morning cleaning the garage with Dad in part because I don't want to be some kind of family-shunning stereotypical snotty teenager. Also because despite that I went out almost every day or night this week, I'm still hoping to see Nadia+Friends tonight. If I'm being a great daughter before band practice, it can only help my cause.

In addition to sweeping the garage floor, I am also keeping a close listen for the *boop* of my text message alert. Ted, you have my number now! Ted, tell me work was canceled and ask me to do something amazing tonight like see Nadia+Friends! With a clean garage, how could the United Front say no?

When I get to practice, Lucy hands each of us lyrics. Reid writes most of our lyrics, but Lucy contributes as well. Then we all work out melodies and rhythms and everything else together.

"Is it cool if we try something with this?" she asks. "I was hoping we could work on it today."

"Sure," Nathan says. "Also I have news."

I feel kind of bad for Lucy with her carefully printed lyrics because suddenly attention is off of her and on Nathan.

"I talked to the Smell's owner," he says. "He liked our demo tracks and said we can open for Murphy-Gomez next month."

A silence washes over us that is the loudest quiet ever. My ears are buzzing with a low hum, but it's almost like maybe they're exploding.

"Are you serious?" Reid finally asks.

"Of course I'm serious," Nathan says.

And then the silence is a long-distant memory, and I can't even tell who's screaming loudest. I do know I am jumping up and down the most and that it looks like Reid might cry and that Lucy is already over losing her moment in the spotlight.

"How did this happen?" Reid asks once the screaming has died down. His tone's the same, I'm positive, as it would be if a spaceship just landed in the room.

"Seriously, guys, I talked to him last time I was there, emailed a link to our site, and it was pretty much it," Nathan says. "This is why I'm saying we need a full EP. If we're getting this much attention just from our demos..."

"You're not in charge, Nathan," Lucy says. Her voice is the sweetest thing next to cotton candy and babies, but she is firm with this.

"I'm not saying I'm in charge," Nathan says. "But—"

"Why are you so obsessed with an EP now?" Lucy asks. "Let's just keep working on making our sets really strong and solid, and getting as many shows as we can. I think that's been working for us."

She looks over to Reid and me like we're supposed to agree, and of course I agree but maybe we shouldn't be picking fights and taking sides and risking how perfect this can be.

"Can we hear your song, Lucy?" I ask.

She smiles at me, the smile that's reserved for Best Friend Riley. It's nice that at least right this very second I can be her again.

We get through practice without any more drama, and afterward Lucy walks right out with the rest of us and tails me right to my car. "Hey, do you want to stay for a while? My mom's bringing home Zankou Chicken later."

"I totally would," I say, "but I planned on doing something after this already."

"Oh," she says.

I can tell she doesn't believe me *BECAUSE IT SOUNDS TOTALLY VAGUE AND MADE UP.*

"Sorry," I say.

"No, I figured you wouldn't want to," she says. "I mean, couldn't. Or, I guess I *do* mean *wouldn't.*"

"I really can't," I say. "And I'd tell you more about what I'm doing, but it would just sound stupid."

Lucy tucks her hair behind her ears and lowers her eyes

to the ground. I realize the guys have already packed up and gone, and it's just the two of us. This is how practice used to end all the time, and sometimes even specifically with Zankou Chicken on the way. I wonder if I didn't already have my next hour all lined up if I'd be tempted to stay. And I wonder if I stayed what it would feel like, if we would sit on her bed juggling plastic containers and yelling at Foley the cat not to jump up to steal chicken. Maybe I'd tell her about Ted and Milo, and maybe even that part could seem a lot like before, when everything between us was easy.

"I never thought anything you said sounded stupid, Riley," she says. "And you should know that."

She heads back in, and even though I wasn't lying, I feel like a jerk. When her garage door goes down I feel the metal descending to the ground is closing things off between us once and for all.

But I still get in my car and drive straight to the Glendale Galleria, where I don't stop in any stores before making my way straight to the food court. Ted is standing behind the counter of Hot Dog on a Stick, true to his word wearing a baseball cap and not the multicolored fez of the girl deep-frying hot dogs and cheese while Ted mans the register. There are people buzzing around, clearly desperate for deep-fried food-court eats, so now that I'm here, I'm not sure what I should be doing.

But then he looks up and notices me. There is a flash over his face like the day was a zero and now it's a ten or five stars or one hundred or whatever ratings system Ted's brain uses.

"Hi, Riley."

"Hi," I say, all casual-like. "Can you fry me some hot dogs?"

"Well, Maribel's working the fryer, but, yeah, I can get you whatever you want," he says, and I have this truly awesome fantasy where I say something like "What I want is to make out with you *RIGHT NOW, TED*," and then he's across the counter and we have a Very Dramatic and Passionate make-out scene right here in the food court.

But I just tell him I would love a hot dog on a stick and the biggest Splenda lemonade they have. He walks over and tells the girl who must be Maribel, who nods and keeps on deep-frying.

"Here." Ted hands me a large lemonade. Our hands touch for a moment, but it's not that sexually charged or anything. There's only so much that you can feel in a food court.

"So you're working until close tonight?" I ask.

"Yeah," he says. "What about you?"

"I don't have anything going on." It's superlame for a Saturday night, but I don't really care. Who wants to scramble around making other plans when standing here at this corn dog and lemonade stand feels like a great time?

"I can take my break soon," he says, "if you want. I mean, to hang out. We could hang out. If you want."

"Yeah," I say, instead of something sexy using the phrase "I want." Man, I am no good at that stuff.

"Cool, give me a few minutes."

Ted joins me almost as soon as I've polished off my food,

and we walk out of the food court toward the main mall. I can't believe he manages to be attractive in his uniform.

"Do you like working in the mall?" I ask, even though I think malls are where hideous people and soul-sucking mainstream crap converge.

"No, it sucks," he says, though cheerfully. "But I had to get a job, so it's fine."

It's the second time he's said he *had to* get a job, and I don't know what exactly it means—like, for money or responsibility or who knows—but what I'm sure of is it doesn't seem like I should ask. Everything between us is so new, and the last thing I want to do is push him.

"What are you up to?"

"I just had practice," I say. "It was fine. We..." I realize I get to share this big thing with him and it's hopefully going to seem like a big thing to him, too. "We're opening for Murphy-Gomez—they're a pretty big local band—at the Smell on a Saturday next month."

"That's awesome, Riley," he says. "Is the Smell a big venue?"

"It's not superbig, but it's really great. It's like an all-ages club, so there isn't any alcohol, and they've given stage time to all these experimental and punk rock bands. Andrew Mothereffing Jackson would play there a lot back when they started out." I stop myself because I could continue for another hour or so with everything cool about the Smell. "It's a really big deal to me."

"I'll make sure I take off work that night so I can go," he says.

"Thank you."

My phone buzzes in my purse, and I probably should just keep doing what I'm doing, which is enjoying the crap out of walking around with Ted, but I check it to see it's a text from Milo: got nadia+friends tix - wanna go?

I look over at Ted, but the truth is, I do want to go. So I go ahead and respond that I have to check with my parents first. It's the least rock-star response possible, after "I'd rather stay home and tend to my antique cup and saucer collection," but it does seem wisest.

"I should get back so I can clock back in on time," Ted says to me.

"Already?" I ask, because it feels like Ted and I have only been hanging out for a few minutes. Then I check the time and realize it's been nearly a half hour. Ted! Don't think I'm clingy! Ted, I just can't keep track of time.

"Unfortunately," he says. "You can text, though. If you want to. I can check my phone sometimes if it's slow."

"Okay," I say. "Bye, Ted."

We lean in just a little, and then we both laugh.

"Just, we're in a mall," he says.

"I *know*," I say. "It's weird."

"I'd kiss you otherwise," he says, and it's crazy how not getting kissed is suddenly the most romantic thing that's ever happened to me.

CHAPTER FORTY-FIVE

<u>The Madison Thing, Continued, by Reid</u>

Things are totally opening up now that I'm dating Madison. Last night she calls while I'm playing <u>Halo</u> and asks if I'm doing anything. I just found an Easter egg that's genius, but this is <u>Madison Price</u>. I save my game and devote full attention to the phone call.

I let her know I'm not doing anything more important than her without making it seem like I'm an antisocial creep without plans. She says there's "sort of a party" going on at Logan Perry's house. I don't jump at inviting myself but really casually say I don't think it would be the worst thing to go. Mom says I can borrow her car so I get it and head over to pick Madison up.

She's waiting in front of her house, and she looked great at school earlier today, but she changed into a dress that's pretty short. I don't know if it's for the party or for me but it can only be a good sign. I don't make a big deal out of how I don't really get invited to this stuff normally and I've never been to a random weeknight party before, and luckily she doesn't either.

We end up messing around in the car for a while instead of going to the party right away. I know Madison used to go out with Ryan Holland and of course apparently every girl's had their expectations set really high by Garrick Bell so I'm feeling a little intimidated but things are going okay.

So when we get to Perry's party I'm in a really good mood. It's exactly the crowd you'd think. Everyone's cool to me, though. I can't believe how big of a deal the show at the fall formal was. People have serious respect for me as a musician, and I'm just instantly accepted as someone who should be at parties like this.

I'm kind of exhausted from all the socializing, which is way more than ever happens for me. Luckily, Madison shows me to an empty room in the house, and we pick up where we left off with the messing around. It's definitely already--in the car--gone further than anything that's happened to me before, which is _awesome_. In all interests of remaining honest I'll say it isn't exactly going _that_ far but for me some new milestones are getting reached.

Then some dude yells and bangs on the door and says Perry's parents are coming home soon so we have to clear out. So we do, and I try to reinitiate things in my car but the moment's pretty much over for both of us plus I'm not sure you can ask a girl to be partially topless in a car so I just take her home.

Still, it's an amazing night, and I think after a couple more like this, we could be to the point of actually doing it. And that's crazy but is starting to feel like something that could actually happen. Obviously, going out with Madison is great--and the possibility of having sex within the near future is great and shocking, considering just very recently everything seemed hopeless.

But I don't know if I should bring it up or just let things happen, and I don't know if I'll be any good at anything. I figured once I was ready to have sex with a girl, things would just be completely awesome. And instead I have all these new things to worry about.

Why does everything have to be so complicated?

CHAPTER FORTY-SIX

On Monday morning, I meet Reid at my locker.

"Hey," he says. "I was walking by Nora Wilton's locker and I heard her saying, 'Can you believe Madison is going out with Reid?'"

"Ugh, Nora Wilton's a jerk," I say. "Who cares?"

"Ri, *who cares*? I care. It's great knowing the whole school is talking about how I don't deserve her. What if she breaks up with me because of that?"

"She won't." Why am I defending Madison Price? Madison Price seems like the kind of person who actually would do that, but I can't have Reid heartbroken. Again. "Seriously, Nora's a huge jerk. You're awesome."

"I'm not awesome," he says. "No one thinks that."

"People think it, Reid. Don't fall apart because of one person."

"I'm not falling apart," he says. "Do I seem like I'm falling apart? Great, that sucks, too. Don't say it so loud people hear you."

"No, and I'm sorry, it sucks if people are saying things like that," I say, because it does. "But you only heard Nora, and like I said, she's like a well-known jerkface. I'm sure no one else is thinking that."

"You don't know that," he says. "Probably everyone else is thinking that."

"I'm serious. They aren't."

I'm sure he doesn't believe me, but at least he seems to accept my belief in this fact and moves on from my locker.

Someone walks up behind me as I'm getting out my chemistry book, and I speak without even moving. "Yes, I mean it."

"You mean what?"

I turn around, and it's actually Madison Price, not Reid, standing there. Ugh.

"Sorry, I thought you were someone else," I say.

"What's up with Reid?" she asks.

"I don't know," I say, instead of "he heard people saying you were too good for him."

"He could barely talk to me this morning," she says.

"He's being weird," I say. "Just, you know, he's neurotic. He needs assurances. Is that stupid to say?"

"No," Madison says, like her whole face is *duh.* "Doesn't everyone?"

"Not like him." I'm afraid it sounds like I'm gossiping. Even though I know Reid is overreacting right now, I still want to protect his fragile ego and heart. "Haven't you noticed that?"

"The other day he did ask me three times what I thought of his shirt, so." She rolls her eyes. "So I guess."

"Yeah, that's it," I say.

She shrugs again. It's, like, her only mode of expression. "Okay."

"He freaks out really easily." Hopefully I'm not stepping over the boundaries of what's okay to say about your friends and what isn't. "But with him it doesn't mean anything. It's just how he exists."

"Okay," she says with another shrug. "Thanks, Riley."

"Hey, um, can I ask you where you got your earring?" I still think it's dumb she wears it, like, every day, but I can admit it's cool.

"Oh, I made it." She reaches up with one hand to fiddle with it. "I can make you one, if you want. It'd look cool when you play."

"Oh, um, thanks." It *will* look cool when I play, and also, maybe Madison is less boring than I thought. At least she's crafty.

"Well, see you." She takes off down the hallway to join up with other girls who are skinny and pretty and rich, because that's how it works, but it's weird how just this fast I don't hate her anymore.

Though she could still stand to learn more expressions and gestures.

* * *

At Yearbook after school, Ted walks in and straight over to me. "Hi, Riley."

"Hey."

We're just kind of standing here beaming at each other in the middle of the back of the room, and I wonder if we seem odd to everyone else. We definitely seem odd to me.

"Oh." Ted opens his messenger bag. I notice the Gold Diggers button I gave him supercasually the other day is pinned in a prominent place. "Aren't these weird?"

He takes out two lollipops and hands both of them to me.

"They're totally normal," I say, but he waves his hands to cut me off.

"No, look at the flavors."

"Bootylicious Blueberry?" I grimace. "Why do people think something named after a butt should go in your mouth?"

"I know!" Ted points to the other one. "That one's weird, too!"

I check the label on the purple lollipop. "Passion...Purple. Not grape?"

"Not grape," he says. *"Purple."*

"You have to eat the Bootylicious one." I pull off the wrapper and hand it to him. He raises his eyebrows but sticks Bootylicious in his mouth. "What does it taste like? Booty?"

He laughs. "No, chemicals. But good chemicals."

"Oh my god, I love chemicals." I shove Passion Purple into my mouth. "These *are* good chemicals."

He sits down at the desk next to my usual desk.

"Are you going to the Past the Heartbreakers show on Friday?" he asks. "I saw your button." He points to it on my bag. "And I've heard they're cool."

"I don't know. Reid hates them, and Milo—" I catch myself. "*My low,* uh, never mind, that doesn't make any sense. Basically I have no one to go with."

"I'm going." He blushes. "I have an extra ticket. For you. I mean, if you want to go. With me."

Oh my god, Ted Callahan is asking me out. For real. On an actual date. To a concert he sought out after memorizing the band buttons on my backpack.

TED IS TOTALLY ASKING ME OUT.

"Totally."

"Okay," he says, "cool."

"I want to taste Bootylicious." I grab the lollipop out of his mouth and swap it with Passion Purple. Oh my god, wait, is this crazy? Sure, we've kissed several times, but maybe it's more intimate to switch lollipops. And Ted raises his eyebrows at me like he knows it's a little strange. Ted, I know it's a little strange, too! I just got all caught up in the asking out and the random flavors, and also I guess I am a little strange!

"Bootylicious is better," he says.

"Is that your professional opinion?" I ask. "As a lollipop expert? Because I totally think Passion Purple is better."

"You don't have to be an expert to recognize its superior quality." Ted swaps the lollipops back. Now we're both weird, so it feels even-grounded, and I'm pretty sure Ted did that just for my benefit.

*   *   *

Reid comes over after school because he claims he needs to talk. I need practice time, but I manage to get in some work on my hand control before Reid lets himself into the guesthouse with Peabody.

"Madison is going to break up with me," he says.

"She isn't." I switch off to a more impressive technique for public consumption. Reid and Peabody count as the public. "She probably thinks *you're* going to break up with *her*, because you're being such a freak."

"'A freak'? Did she say that?"

"God, *NO*. Stop it, Reid. She's pretty and popular and apparently good at crafts or at least feather arts so just *ACCEPT IT*."

He stares at me for a solid minute. "What are feather arts?"

"Never mind, just, Reid, she's into you." My phone buzzes, again, from the floor. I grab for it and grin at the screen. *Ted Callahan calling.*

"Who is it?" Reid asks. *LIKE HE KNOWS.*

"No one," I say. "My dad."

Why did I say that! It is so clearly not my dad from the goofy face I'm making. But I don't want to take a potentially romantic call with Ted right in front of Reid, so I do something tragic: I send Ted to voice mail.

216

"Ted was cute to me earlier," I say, testing the topic.

"How?"

I tell him about the lollipops because this is news I want to share with *someone*. To be honest, the best audience for the story would be Lucy, but that isn't an option right now.

Reid makes a face. "That seems unhygienic."

"It's no more unhygienic than kissing," I say, even though that's just a guess and not a scientific fact.

"I guess not." Reid shrugs. "Just tell me what to do about Madison."

"Just be happy. Can't you do that?"

He stares at me, and I realize maybe he can't. There's a cool and pretty and potentially-actually-interesting girl who *likes him*, and he's all caught up in disastrous possibilities instead of the awesome reality right in front of him. But even though I've now at least sort of dated three guys, and the whole romance world seems less foreign, I don't know how to fix this for him. Instead I invite him to stay for dinner because it's really the only thing within my power right now.

CHAPTER FORTY-SEVEN

<u>The Madison Thing, Continued, by Reid</u>

Madison's hanging out with me after school near my locker, like, almost every day, and she asks if she can come over after school and hang out.

    I don't know what to do because:

<u>PROS:</u>

1. Obviously a girl wanting to come over to your place is a good sign about sex or at least sex-related things.
2. Our house is pretty nice and Mom has all these impressive awards on the mantel in the living room.
3. Probably if she wanted to dump me she'd have no problem doing it in public

or over the phone or something, so I have at least another day of dating her I figure.

CONS:

1. If I had known a girl was going to be in my room later, I would have cleaned it entirely, like a spring-cleaning-level cleaning, with fresh sheets and a new Glade PlugIn in my outlet.

2. Also obviously I would have put away some of the board games on my shelf and maybe a third of the framed animation cells Mom got me when I was younger that are still pretty freaking awesome and will be worth a lot of money someday.

3. Peabody's still getting used to living in a house and occasionally has an accident. It's not a big deal, but it doesn't seem very romantic to walk a girl into a house where a dog just pooped.

4. As Riley is well aware, Mom has all these childhood photos of me littered

throughout the house like I'm a saint or celebrity (of Michael, too, but the ones of me are objectively more embarrassing), and I'd like to remove at least 60 percent of them.

But I really can't say no to Madison (seriously, I'm not sure it's possible scientifically) so she follows me over to my house. Peabody earns extra treats because there aren't any accidents anywhere in the house, and it turns out Madison actually really likes dogs and we head out on the longest walk I've ever taken with Peabody so far. We try and stop at one point that's on kind of a secluded stretch of sidewalk to kiss, but apparently kissing makes Peabody bark so we give up on that. (Thanks a lot, Peabody.)

When we get back to the house, for some reason Mom is home weirdly early but it's cool because I've already told her all about Madison and she doesn't act embarrassing, though Madison does ask a lot of questions about the worst of the pictures of me. Mom answers all the questions and she and Madison are developing, like, this witty banter thing. I haven't been able to relax enough around Madison to develop anything like that so it's really frustrating that my mom is so cool.

So what I'm saying is no matter what good things happen, I'm sure this is still pretty much doomed.

CHAPTER FORTY-EIGHT

Madison walks up to me again a couple days later while I'm fighting books in and out of my locker. Maybe I should ask Ted to install a shelf for me. "Hey."

"Hey," I say.

"Here," she says, and shoves a little box at me. The box is covered with this filmy metallic paper, and when I open it up there's a feather earring inside, just like she said she'd make for me. It's greenish blue and looks nothing like hers, so we won't be creepy earring twins. "If you don't like it, whatever, I can make you a different one."

"No, it's awesome. Thank you! I like the box, too."

She shrugs. "I also made the box."

"Oh my god, the box is even cooler than the earring! And the earring is awesome to begin with."

Madison shrugs again. "Okay. You're welcome."

Ted walks down the hallway and waves, and I try not to grin beyond an appropriate manner as he walks up. "Hi, Riley."

Madison shrugs again and heads off down the hall.

"What's in the box?" Ted asks.

"This." I take out the earring and put it in. "It's a cool box, right?"

"Definitely, yeah." He places something in the palm of my hand. "I have to get to class. See you in world history."

"See you then." I look down to see a tiny box of jelly beans. Score! Jewelry and candy in one morning.

Garrick smiles and waves at me as I walk into class. "Hi, Riley!"

"Hey." I sit down next to him and open my book.

"Can I have one of those?" Garrick asks me, and I feel myself raring up to exclaim my shock over such a request. Except I remember that Garrick doesn't know these are jelly beans of love. So I give him some.

I get a text from Milo as I'm walking to lunch, with news that Purple & Black is playing a free set at Amoeba tonight. So I respond with a **yeahhh c u there!!!**

After band practice that night I rush home, and—luckily?—Mom and Dad are both there already. I sit down at the kitchen table with my homework *LIKE I NEVER DO* and hope it gives me an air of industrious responsibility, not suspicion.

Dad leans over my world history textbook. "What are you learning in this?"

"Blah blah, the Romans," I say. "Hey, guys, would it be okay if I went to a show at Amoeba tonight? I'll come home right after."

"Riley," Mom says, "this week you had Yearbook and band practice. One night Reid was over, Monday you stopped off somewhere on your way home, and I'm sure you have plans Friday night." *(DO I!)* "Would it kill you to spend the rest of the evening here?"

"But Purple & Black, this band I like, is doing a free set," I say. "I've never seen them live, and, again, it's free."

"They're pretty good," Dad says. "Like Tegan and Sara but less Canadian."

"Yes!" I feel bad for not going into more detail with him on the Romans. "So is it okay?"

There's a lot of heavy sighing from the United Front as Ashley sweeps into the room to get yogurt from the refrigerator. "Is Riley going out again? Riley's *always* going out."

Killing your sister should be a thing you can do, if you want.

"No," Dad says. "Riley, I'm sorry."

"Seriously?"

"Seriously," Mom or Dad or whatever member of the United Front says.

I leave my books on the kitchen table and run out to the guesthouse where I call Milo.

"Hey." His voice is full of promise and upcoming concert-going.

"Hi, I'm sorry, I know this is so superlame, but my parents are being stupid and I'm not allowed to go out tonight, and I'm really sorry."

"That sucks," he says. "Is there any way you can sneak out?"

Sneak out? I'd never even thought of that. I am seriously the worst rock star ever.

"Yes," I say, even though I have no plan of attack. It's going to be *SO GOOD* to document later in the Passenger Manifest, and also I don't want to pass up this show. Milo promises to pick me up down the street so Mom and Dad won't see or hear his car, and I act disappointed and pathetic at dinner as to not set off any alerts.

After dinner I go back out to the guesthouse and crank up my iPod hooked to my speakers and let it run as I walk down the street. Milo's car is there, as promised. I am a freaking certified badass as I sit down in the passenger seat. Milo's blond hair has been cut since I saw him last, and it's spiking up just a little, like he's a tough guy who doesn't care too much about his gorgeous freaking hair.

"That was actually supereasy," I say. "Thanks for picking me up."

He leans over to kiss me. "Thanks for going with me."

"Thanks for telling me about it," I say.

"I know I can rely on you for show attendance," Milo says with a grin. "How's everything with the band?"

I start to tell him about our gig at the Smell, but I know Ted's going, and that feels too dangerous. "Well, Nathan hasn't mentioned the EP or his epic riches as much lately, so I guess they're okay."

I feel like I'm cheating on Ted, but, after all, Ted is not my boyfriend. Ugh, Ted! He's working hard at deep-frying corn dogs and sticks of cheese while I'm out with this other guy. I feel like I'm maybe a jerk, so I get out my phone to text him.

i wish u could come to p&b show w/ me!!

Ted texts back a few minutes later. Milo and I aren't talking much because we're blasting the Feelies and singing along. Me too! Have fun. Don't get anything weird signed. I grin to myself and text back. like what? a puppy? He takes a bit to respond and I remind myself he's making lemonades and fried foods. I meant like a body part. But not a puppy either. Marker ink's probably bad for puppies.

"Everything cool?" Milo asks me. "Your parents aren't onto you, are they?"

"No, free and clear," I say. "It's just my friend Reid."

Why am I lying?

My phone buzzes again, and this time it *is* Reid.

Madison says I'm acting weird and things are cool. I know she's lying!

"Do you have friends you wish you could punch?" I ask Milo.

"Definitely," he says. "Some people need it."

"I can't even text him back over this," I say. "Oh, wait, no, I can, I have an icon of a fist I can send. Do you think that's clear?"

Milo laughs. "It's pretty clear."

So I text back the fist, and Reid responds in a flash. He is not Ted with his endless other responsibilities. **Is that a fist bump or a fist punch?**

"I guess it wasn't clear enough," I say aloud, which makes Milo laugh again.

Once we get to Amoeba, there's a crowd already inside crowding the stage that's been set up for the night. But Milo and I are experts at this. We slide through the empty spaces and get right up front for Purple & Black's set.

"Do you want to get something signed?" Milo asks me after the set. "Or should we take off?"

"No, I do," I say, dashing over to get in line.

"I'm, um, I'm going to get something for this friend of mine who couldn't come tonight." I lean against a CD bin to appear casual.

Milo raises an eyebrow. Do I not seem casual enough? I lean harder.

"Okay," he says.

So I ask Macy (vocals and guitar) and Lyndel (vocals and piano) to sign their newest CD for Ted, who is stuck at Hot Dog on a Stick, and they do, and I grin down at this perfect present for the guy who gives me candy and mix CDs. If he hasn't heard of Purple & Black, I hope he'll like them anyway.

"Who's Ted?" Milo asks me. "Is he the other guy in your band?"

"No, that's Nathan. Ted's just this guy, um, in Yearbook with me. He's always stuck at his job."

When Milo parks a block from my house, I'm so nervous about making it back in unseen that I just thank him and wave and jump out really fast like I'm rolling to safety from a moving vehicle. I should have changed clothes earlier so I'd be wearing all black like a ninja or cat burglar or heist type, but I'm in red Chucks and jeans and a yellow Ted Leo and the Pharmacists hoodie. It's a stupid sneaky outfit, but I walk right into the guesthouse and my music is still playing and it's like I never left. Holy crap. I just got away with something.

I spend a few minutes in here before heading inside, where Mom and Dad are watching some TV procedural about solving murders. They barely glance up at me, and I say good night and walk upstairs like a champion liar. Wait, no, that's horrible. I don't want to be a champion liar.

I text Milo to let him know the sneaking out was a success, and he seems happy about this (**Nice work! c u soon**), so I guess we're okay even after the weird moment when I got the CD signed for Ted. Anyway, that moment would only prove Reid semi-right, so I don't mention it at all when I log my badass night in the Passenger Manifest, even though I'm still thinking about it. I wonder how I'd feel if Milo had gotten a CD signed for a girl who isn't me. Still, for the Passenger Manifest, I leave things 100 percent badass.

*   *   *

I make my way to Ted's locker the next morning and try to figure out whatever magical method he used to maneuver a CD into my locker. The Purple & Black CD is even in one of those slim cardboard jackets, but I can't figure out how he did it. I'm probably pointlessly cycling through all my previous fruitless methods when I feel a hand on my shoulder.

I spin around with a smile because it'll seem adorable to Ted that he caught me red-handed. But it is definitely *NOT* Ted; it's Mrs. Bullard, whose classroom is right by Ted's locker, and I'm pretty sure she doesn't think I'm adorable.

"Miss Crowe-Ellerman," she says, "I know that this is not your locker."

"Oh, I know, too, I was just trying to..." I hold up the CD like it will speak all necessary words of explanation for me. CD, do my bidding! "It's a gift!"

"You know the student handbook policy on tampering with other students' lockers," she says, which is not true. I am not at all aware of pretty much anything in the student handbook.

"I'm not tampering," I say, even though I was trying to bend the metal air vents with the superhero force of my powerful biceps. "Okay, it's tampering, but I was tampering out of—"

OH MY GOD I ALMOST SAID "LOVE"!

Ted rounds the corner and smiles when he sees me. "Hi, Riley."

"Mr. Callahan," Mrs. Bullard says. "Miss Crowe-Ellerman was tampering with your locker."

"No, it's okay," he says quickly. "She's my—"

I hold my breath to see what I am. But Ted's face just gets bright red, and he says nothing. In fact he is so quiet it's like he is subtracting all the speech from the world.

"All right," Mrs. Bullard says. "Miss Crowe-Ellerman, I suggest you review your student handbook."

"I totally will," I say.

"I have one in my locker she can borrow," Ted says as Mrs. Bullard walks back into her classroom. "Wow, that was really dramatic."

"I'm so sorry! I was just trying to leave you this." I give him the CD, and he grins at it, then at me. "I wish you could have come."

"Me too, but, thanks, Riley, this is great." He leans in and *OH MY GOD, IS TED GOING TO KISS ME IN THE SCHOOL HALLWAY RIGHT BY MRS. BULLARD'S ROOM, AND HOW MANY STUDENT HANDBOOK POLICIES WILL THAT VIOLATE?*

But all he does is put his hand on my forearm.

"See you in world history," I say, because as much as I want to stand here having my arm touched, I need to get to my locker.

"Okay." Ted waves and heads off.

When I get to my locker, he has already tampered with it, because I have a fun-size Milky Way. This is a good day.

Reid catches up with me right as I'm about to walk into chemistry. "Ri, emergency."

"What." I try my best, but I can't make it sound like a question. Everything in Reid's life lately is an emergency.

"I wrote it in this." He shoves the Passenger Manifest into my purse. "But I just have to say it. Last night I went over to Madison's, and I guess things are okay."

"Good!" I say. "Also that doesn't sound like an emergency."

"I haven't gotten to the emergency part yet. So we were up in her room and started messing around, which is, as you know, way more than what's happened so far. Like, things are moving along—"

"How far?" I ask.

"Like, second-and-a-half base," he says.

I have no idea what that could even mean. "What are you talking about?"

"It's, you know, it's more than second," Reid says.

"But what does that mean?"

"Ri, this is an emergency!" Reid clears his throat. "So, okay, if you were making out with a guy and it wasn't good, would you let him know?"

"Dude," I say, even though I'm not sure I've ever called Reid *dude* before. "Can you for once not assume that something awful is going on? I can tell things with you and Madison are great."

"Would you stop and say, 'Hey, Reid, that wasn't good'?"

"No, I totally wouldn't." I stare at him. "Oh my god. Did she say that to you?"

"No! No. *NO.*" He musses up his hair a bunch. "Just, what if I wasn't good at any of it? What if today she's telling people that? Or deciding never to see me again?"

"Reid, I'm sure she's not."

"Ri, second-and-a-half base is a big deal."

"*I HAVE NO IDEA WHAT YOU EVEN MEAN,*" I say. "Sorry. Just, I know it is, but unless she was acting repulsed, you have nothing to worry about, I'm sure."

"How would I know if she was acting repulsed?"

"Reid! You would Just Know."

"Actually... I've been wondering something, Ri."

I manage not to sigh really loudly and yell *WHAT?* "Yes?"

"Not that we've put any requirements on it, but do you realize you've never mentioned anything to do with Milo—"

"Don't say his name aloud."

"Whatever. You've never mentioned anything to do with him in the Passenger Manifest."

"Obviously I have," I say. "Meeting him at Amoeba, remember? And our first date or whatever at the Atwater farmers' market, and my ID, and—"

"You know what I mean," Reid says, and I don't. "Have you even kissed him?"

"*OF COURSE I HAVE,*" I say. "A lot!"

"Really," he says instead of asks.

"Have I actually not mentioned it?" I think about this for a moment, as those kisses creep into my brain. "I guess I haven't. Ugh. Reid. It's not good."

"See?" Reid waves his arms around, and I think it's supposed to look triumphant. "This is what I'm worried about."

"There's nothing *wrong* with him," I say. "We just don't have the right chemistry or something. I'm sure it's different for you and Madison."

"But you said I'd just know. Does Mi—does *he* Just Know?"

I think of how Milo always grins before he kisses me. It's not his smooth cool rock-and-roll grin; it's something purer and sweeter in those moments. "Fine. I guess he doesn't." I start backing into my classroom to get away from the conversation as well as thoughts of pure and sweet Milo. "But you guys aren't the same, and this is not an emergency. Okay?"

"We're talking more about this later." He waves his finger at me like he's a sassy mom.

"I'm sure we will."

CHAPTER FORTY-NINE

Tips for Guys on Making Out with Girls (WHICH REID IS FORCING ME TO WRITE), by Riley

1. Fresh, minty breath is good.
2. Don't use too much pressure, you are not vacuuming her mouth.
3. Biting can be sexy but also it can just be crazy painful, so use your teeth thoughtfully.
4. Don't slobber. She shouldn't have to wipe off her face afterward.
5. Your tongue's not a probe.
6. Lip balm isn't for girls only, so use it.
7. Do the thing where you make your lips soft but also powerful in a good way.
8. Don't be all specific-body-parts-focused. Touch her hair and face and shoulders, too.

9. If you want stuff done, you'd better be willing to do stuff.
10. Just FYI, we know when you're accidentally touching our boobs and when you're "accidentally" touching our boobs.

CHAPTER FIFTY

I pick Ted up at six after school on Friday. He emerges from his apartment complex in a button-down shirt and jeans and his usual Chucks. It's nicer than what he wore today, just like my outfit—a bright stripey shirt, my best jean skirt, tights, and my black boots—is way nicer than anything I normally wear to school.

"Hi, Riley," he says as he gets into my car. Hopefully it's not strange I'm playing the CD he made for me. "Do you want to get dinner? There's this cool place in Sunset Junction, Flore. It's vegan but it's good, I mean, I'm not a vegan, and I like it."

"No, Flore is great," I say. "Do you think a vegan could work at Hot Dog on a Stick or would that be ethically compromised?"

"Probably it'd be ethically compromised." He laughs. "Hey, um, I'm glad you could go tonight."

"I'm really glad you asked me," I say. I crank up the Super-chunk song that's playing on the CD, and by the time we get to Flore, I am full of smiles and laughter and a bunch of other probably annoying things. Being around Ted does this to me.

We talk the whole time, about how Mr. Heckart and Mrs. Bullard clearly are having an affair, how it seems possible that Wild Flag will never put out another record, but at least they've given the world one nearly flawless one (well, I lead that conversation, but Ted seems super-interested), how for some reason the courtyard at the school always smells like doughnuts but we have never witnessed a doughnut in the vicinity.

All of a sudden we realize it's nearly eight, and Ted pays the bill despite my protests. Since I can tell he's trying to be a gentleman, it's sort of sweet. We race outside and I speed down Sunset like a champion race-car driver, though champion race-car drivers don't have to keep circling different blocks in search of parking. Finally I wedge my car into a spot, and Ted and I run inside.

The first opener, I'm Listening, is already playing, so we run right into the crowd. Their set is loud and fast, and we don't stop jumping up and down until between songs. We chug a bunch of water afterward and fight our way back to the front for Fawnskin. The club has filled up by the time their set is over, so Ted and I stay firmly planted where we are in anticipation of Past the Heartbreakers.

"Thanks for getting these tickets," I tell him.

"I really wanted to go," he says, "with you."

It is the perfect moment to kiss him, but then Past the Heartbreakers take the stage. So I scream along with the whole crowd and get swept away in the noise and rhythm and heat. Ted may not have a lot of music cred, but it doesn't matter. At a show he's perfect.

After the second encore ends, we walk out of the hot, muggy club and into the crisp night. I'm afraid Ted's phone will beep or his mom will pull up or Reid will appear in a poof of smoke and sparks with his latest emergency, and I'm not ready for any of tonight to be over.

"Do you have to go home?" I ask him.

"No," he says. "I mean, not now. Not *not ever.*"

I lace my fingers through his, and he pulls me in. I think about waiting for him to make the next move, but for Ted I think the pulling-me-in is the next move. So I kiss him, even though we're on the sidewalk in public. Ted's lips move against mine. It's soft, slow kissing that gives off white noise in my brain that shuts everything else out. Ted tastes like lemon drops.

"Let's go to my car," I say, not because I care about anyone else's sensibilities who has to watch us, but because I want all of this to just be for Ted and me. But once we get in my car, we get distracted picking out music for the drive back and forget to start kissing again.

I love how Ted is trying so hard with music.

We end up back at my house because I have no working knowledge of wherever people park their cars to make out. But when I lean over the center console to head back into Kissing Ted Land, the motion detector light on the front porch goes off. Now we're both so bright.

"Do you want to see my practice space?" I ask. It's a twofold thing, where I do want to show Ted my drums, but also I have this private guesthouse, and it's the perfect place to make out with someone. Kissing Ted Callahan is one thing, and it's a dramatic and amazing and mystical thing on its own. Making out with him is going to be something else entirely.

He follows me into the backyard where I get fumbly with the keys before I manage to let us in. Technically, I don't think I'm supposed to have people in here alone late at night, but the United Front has never specifically said so, so I'm not breaking any rules. Technically.

There is no time for the drums now that we're here, though, and I don't even know who kisses who first, and I stop keeping track of anything along those lines.

Ted is kissing me with urgency, with his hands holding my face, skimming around my waist, tracing lines down my back. It's like there's no more oxygen, and all I can breathe now is Ted and him me. Our teeth keep getting mixed up with each other's lips, and I am kind of shocked at myself, how I could devour Ted Callahan. I'm sure I was good at stuff before, but I am great at stuff with Ted.

We keep finding new spaces to lean against while kissing, like there aren't enough places to contain this to. Ted pushes me against the wall, I'm leaning him into the door, we're maybe not leaning on anything but each other because it's like the world will end if we can't line up every inch of ourselves with one another. Finally I'm tired of these balancing acts and pull Ted to the floor with me, and it is a first, this thing where I'm lying down and kissing a guy who is next to me, and then under me, and then over me. Who knew that a guy who could start out so timid would end up kissing you with this intensity like he'd been thinking about it for as long as you have.

"Do you want to stop?" I ask, because I feel like I'm supposed to check in with him at some point.

"No," he says automatically.

It is the best no I've ever heard.

"Unless you do. Do you?" He's already sitting up. "We can stop."

"We can't," I say, because it is the best line I can think of, and also because the feelings that buzzed through me all the times I dreamed of this happening are so much stronger now that it actually is.

I get up and shimmy out of my jacket before throwing my iPod into its dock (not that the silence was bad). Ted takes off his hoodie, too, and then it's like the barriers have given way for clothes needing to stay on. My shirt off, Ted's shirt off, Ted's pants off, my skirt and tights off, *pow*. Ted is like all the boys in dumb books about teenagers and can't figure out how to get my bra off, but I'm well versed in that, so we're fine.

Ted starts laughing, which, despite how much I love Ted's laugh, is not exactly what I want to hear when I am PG-13 naked. "What are you wearing?"

It is obvious I did not think this night would turn into

This Night, because I am wearing Day of the Week under-wear printed with cartoon frogs, and also, they're not even the right day. They are Tuesday.

"What do frogs even have to do with *Tuesdays?*" he asks.

"Frogs love Tuesdays, duh," I say, and we crack up.

"Do you want to stop?" he asks. I feel like exclaiming to the heavens, "Ted clearly wants to do me right now!" but I don't because it'll be way better if instead of talking about it, it just happens.

And.

It.

Just.

Happens.

In movies, there's always soft lighting and cuddling right after, but we are on the floor of a dark, unfurnished guest-house. Also, I think we're both surprised about what just went on. I'm surprised, at least, and in the moonlight Ted's eyes look very wide.

"You should go home," I say. "I mean, because it's late. Not because I want you to—"

"Yeah, curfew, exactly," Ted says.

"Ted," I say.

"Riley," he says, like we're doing a bit.

"That was, like, a new thing." *IT IS THE WEIRDEST WAY TO REFER TO SEX EVER.*

"Yeah," he says. "For me, too."

I want to tell him so much, like that I'm so glad it was with him and that for him it was with me, and that there's so much about him that's cute, and that I had condoms in my purse because I got them free at a booth I walked by at a health fair, not because I was out on the prowl for dudes.

Actually, I guess I've been out on the prowl for dudes for a while. It's just that Ted is one specific dude who matters.

But I don't say any of that because in my brain it's scattered enough. If I try to verbalize it, who knows the torrential downpour of words that might rain from my mouth. And I don't want to ruin this super-perfect nice moment. Also he must know! Well, not specifically the health fair part, but the rest.

We get dressed and walk outside, and I drive him home and park where there is no motion detector light, so we spend a few minutes in the car kissing. It's soft and slow again, which is funny that we could end up back here after what just happened.

I'm glad we can.

"See you Monday," Ted says. "I'm working tomorrow. But you can come by if you want."

"I'll totally come by," I say, and not just because Ted in his uniform is a glorious vision. "See you then."

"See you, Riley."

On my way home I crank the CD in my stereo and sing along, even though after screaming at the concert I shouldn't have much of a voice left. I am a girl who's had sex. This changes *everything*. At home I even look in the mirror because a thing like this should be apparent. I even stare myself down like a master supervillain in one of Mom and Dad's beloved spy movies.

But, no, I look exactly the same. So if it's not this huge life-changing, course-altering event, what the heck does that mean about installing a wall of silence between Lucy and me?

I don't want to think about any of that. I am going to enjoy every single last awesome bit of tonight.

CHAPTER FIFTY-ONE

The Madison Thing, Continued, by Reid

Madison calls me after school and says her dad and stepmom are going to be out, so I should come over. I know this is a very good sign. It's such a good sign, I bring, to be polite, precautions. If you're wondering why I had precautions handy, it's thanks to the health fair.

So I get there and I was kinda hoping Madison would give me some really clear sign, like opening the door wearing something like underwear, but she's wearing the same thing she wore to school. Also she ordered Thai food, which doesn't seem like she's planning an evening of romance. Though I will say the Thai's from Bulan and it's really good.

So Madison says she heard something about me, and I start sweating and shaking but I'm trying to act like I'm not, and I have no idea what she could have heard but I doubt there are any really solid pro-Reid Goodwin rumors. And apparently what she heard--and I have no idea from who--is that I am really good at Scrabble.

How is there a rumor that I am really good at Scrabble? Where did that start? I can't stop trying to figure it out, and I'm waiting for her to kick me out because it's probably not a very attractive quality in a guy. But she says she's secretly awesome at Scrabble and plans to kick my ass.

I do my best to use romantic or sexy words, but the best I can manage is getting O, R, and A when there's an L to play off of, but it seems tacky and gross so I don't. I try to analyze Madison's plays for any kind of subliminal messages, but it's just a bunch of random smart Scrabble moves that make words like qi and jammy, so I'm getting nothing there.

The game takes a really long time and Madison actually is a secret Scrabble wizard, and she doesn't completely demolish me but she does end up beating me, and at that point I'm kind of exhausted but I'm still trying to think of a good move to make, like, on her, not the game--by now the game's over. She just says we should go up to her room, and I am really glad I brought precautions, but then the front door opens and her parents walk in, and Madison's just all, "See ya, Reid," and waves good-bye to me.

So I still haven't had sex and also I am no longer the best at Scrabble at Edendale High. Tonight was a big loss.

(Okay I might be being dramatic. Madison did end up walking me to my car and we kissed for at least eight minutes.)

CHAPTER FIFTY-TWO

At practice the next day I try to walk in like I always do, but part of me wants to swagger, and part of me doesn't even want to look at Lucy or Reid. Or, I guess, Nathan either.

"Can we start with 'Can't Talk' again?" Lucy asks. "I'd really like it to be ready for the Smell."

"Totally," I say. "Reid, are you tuned? Can we go?"

"Ri, it's a delicate process," he says.

I turn to roll my eyes at Lucy, but she looks away. Yikes.

No, my post-doing-it-with-Ted-Callahan mood is not to be ruined. I count off with my sticks, and we launch into "Can't Talk." We play it over and over until it's shaping up, and we work awhile on an Andrew Mothereffing Jackson cover and run through "Tease," "Garage," "Holly Trueheart," "Across the Room," and "Tone Deaf." I'm hoping to have all this new-found sexually charged drumming or rhythm power, but I'm exactly the same, even though I am Riley Jean Crowe-Ellerman, Virgin No More.

"Can you guys practice awhile later today?" Nathan asks.

"We could get even more done if we keep going, and we'll be in better shape for our show."

He's right, but if I leave now, I still have time to see Ted before going home to have dinner with the United Front. "Um, maybe this is enough for today?"

Wait, what am I doing?

"No, never mind, you're right, Nathan, of course, as always," I say, which is bitchier than anything I am actually thinking. "Sorry, I just—let's keep going."

"Is that supposed to mean something?" Nathan asks.

"No, god, sorry, I'm having a weird day. Can we keep playing?"

Everyone looks back at me like I'm a circus freak, but we do keep going. By the time we finish, Nathan suggests we walk to Best Fish Taco, but I feel panicky about time, so after carrying my drums out to my car I wave good-bye and drive off.

At this point I should probably just go straight home, but I head to the Galleria and run into the food court. Ted is watching a bunch of corn dogs fry in intense concentration, but I walk right up and wave.

"Hi, Ted."

"Hi, Riley," he says with a grin. "Hey."

"Hey." I laugh and watch as his face turns red. Oh my god, he's the cutest. "I'm sure you're superbusy, but I wanted to say hi."

Oh my god, we have now said *hi* or *hey*, like, twenty-seven times each.

"How was practice?" he asks.

"Really good. We're trying to play everything a ton so we're ready for the Smell. How's work?"

"Busy." He gestures to the bubbling frying foods. "I can't take a break for a while. I'm really sorry."

"It's totally okay. Just, I have this thing I have to do with my parents, is all, so I can't hang around too long."

"It's fine," Ted says. "I'll call you when I get off. I have to go home because it'll be late, and I was out late last night, but—"

"Yes, call me." I don't know how to say good-bye, because I really want to kiss him and of course I can't. So I wave, and he waves back, and then I go home, where I'll try to act enthused about dinner, even though really I'll just be counting down until Ted's off work and can call me.

* * *

On Monday morning I'm not sure how I can act like a normal person when Ted walks toward my locker. We grin at each other, and I hug him because I'm so washed over with happy Ted thoughts I forget I don't want Reid to see us. Of course, I'll end things with Milo when I get the chance, but I'll worry about that later. There's nothing but Ted I want to think about today.

Still, I pull it together and act like my usual self for the rest of the day. After seventh period I wait by Ted's locker and force myself not to tackle him as he walks up.

"Hi, Riley."

"Hi." I grin like we are in on the best inside joke the world has to offer. I get why Lucy and Nathan are so annoying. "Do you want to hang out?"

"Now?" he asks.

"Yeah, now," I say. "Do you have work?"

"I'm free, yeah, we can hang out," he says.

"My little sister's going to be home," I say.

"No one's home at my apartment," he says. "Not for a while at least."

"Okay." I wait as he takes almost every book out of his locker. It seems like Ted is taking twenty classes instead of seven. "Do you really have that much homework?"

"Yeah?" He laughs like I'm funny, which I love. "I just want to make sure if I want to study I can."

He is dedicated and nerdy and it's awesome.

I drive to his apartment, and as he lets me in I think about how this is the first time I'm going inside and not just dropping him off at the door. It's crazy that not long ago he was just a guy I obsessed over and now this is a real thing. *We're* a real thing.

"Do you want soda or something?" he asks as soon as we're through the door. I'm too busy looking around to think about beverages yet. Everyone else I know lives in a house and not an apartment. But now that I'm inside it seems just like anyone else's place: cozy, with family photos and certificates of achievement framed on the walls.

I sit on the overstuffed green couch while Ted gets us

Cokes, and he sits down next to me and turns the TV on to *Blind Love.*

"This one is great." Ted points to the TV. "He falls in the hot tub at some point. His blindfold gets all wet and stuck to his face, but he can't take it off."

"Oh my god, I haven't seen it." I love that he watches this show and remembers I watch it, too.

The episode is as good as Ted promised, but of course I'm also thinking about sex and if it's going to happen again and how I'd really like it to happen again. And then as soon as the episode's over Ted kisses me and it's like I Just Know.

We stay on the couch kissing for a while, but once the clothes-coming-off stage arrives, Ted leads me down the hallway to his room, and this time is way better. Last time was amazing in that it was amazing that it happened, but right now is less awkward and uncomfortable, and of course it's nicer being in Ted's bed versus the guesthouse. And I planned ahead today; my underwear is plain and black and normal! It still came in a three-pack Mom bought me at Target, but it's a move up from the Tuesday frogs. The condom also flummoxes us way less this time, and we seem like we're lined up better or something.

Also somehow I like Ted even more than I did only three days ago.

Afterward we get dressed right away just in case we lose track of time and his mom gets home. Ted wants to go back to the living room and watch TV, but I have to be nosy and look around his room first. He has an FYF Fest poster tacked up, and a framed old-fashioned drawing of trains. I notice then there are also a couple of miniature trains on top of his bookcase, which is full of classics and graphic novels and essay books by smart-ass people.

"What's with the trains?" I ask.

"I don't know—I used to be into trains," he says. "It's geeky, I know."

"Everyone's geeky in some way."

"My dad used to buy them for me," he says. "When I was little. Our house had this small basement, and he set up a track to run around the whole thing. It was pretty cool."

I haven't ever asked anything about the pronounced lack of a dad in Ted's life, since there are things like Reid's dad living in Chicago and having that be no big deal because he calls a lot and they FaceTime while watching the Cubs play on TV. But I guess sometimes it can be a big deal.

"Sounds cool," I say in a voice I hope isn't sarcastic. "Where's your dad now? If it's okay I asked! Sorry if I shouldn't have—"

"Riley, it's okay," he says, but there's a note of something in his voice that makes me put my hand on his arm like he needs steadying. "He died three years ago."

"Oh," I say. It is all I know to say to him. It must have happened right before high school, because we didn't go to middle school together, and I hate that I didn't know this fact about Ted Callahan, and I hate that I don't have more to say to him now.

"Yeah," he says.

And I somehow know it's all he can say, too. I give him a hug, and he leans into it really snug. It's nice to feel like you're exactly enough for what someone needs.

"Anyway, I know trains are kind of dorky, but I still like them."

I should tell him I like that he's a dork, but it doesn't sound like a compliment, so I say nothing instead. "Do you want to go to the Unacknowledged Parrot show on Friday? I think you'd like them. I can send you some MP3s."

"I have work," he says, "but I think I'll get off in time. I can meet you there if that's okay."

"It's totally okay, yeah." My phone buzzes in my pocket, and when I take it out, I see that it's Milo calling. Bad timing, Milo!

"Are you okay?" Ted asks.

I realize I am wearing the expression of a reaction shot in a movie about diseases. "Fine, sure, yes, sorry."

"Let's go watch TV." He takes my hand and gets me out of his trains room. After a couple more episodes of *Blind Love*, Ted's mom calls and lets him know she's running late. Obviously, we head back to his room to do it again.

It's late by then, and I figure Mom and Dad are annoyed with me, but I text and say I'm studying with a friend from

Yearbook—only partially a lie—and we order a pizza. I could sit with Ted watching dumb TV and eating delicious cheesy pizza and messing around forever, but after the pizza's gone, I kiss him good night and go home.

I dig around in my purse for the Passenger Manifest while I'm checking my email in my room—awesome, Ted has sent me a YouTube clip of the hot-tub fall—and can't find it. After a couple of viewings of the clip, I turn my full attention to my purse and, still, it's nowhere to be found.

"Crap," I say aloud. A cold sweat appears on the back of my neck, like the time I came down with the flu out of nowhere. I dump out the contents of my bag, and while I locate my missing lip balm, there is no notebook.

Oh, it's probably just that Rcid took it without asking. Yes! He's gotten very comfortable with the contents of my bag. I grab my phone from the pile of discarded purse stuff and call him.

"Yo," he says.

"*STOP DOING THAT.* So you have the Passenger Manifest, right?"

"Uh, no."

"You're sure?"

"Yeah, I'm positive."

"Reid," I say. My heart is pounding in every single part of my body, and not in the good, sexy way. My mouth tastes like foil. "It's gone."

"You're sure?" he asks in a calm voice. "Did you check your purse?"

"*OF COURSE I CHECKED MY PURSE,*" I say. "*WHY WOULDN'T I CHECK MY PURSE.*"

"Okay, okay," he says. "What about your backpack?"

"No. Good idea." I unzip it and dump out its contents. There is no notebook, though I do find the granola bar I thought I lost last week. "Wait, check *your* backpack. Just to be safe."

"Hang on." There's a long pause and then the sound of a bunch of stuff hitting the floor. "No. What about your locker?"

I let relief wash away all the heart-pounding and foil-tasting and faux-flu-having. "I'm sure it's there."

It's never been anywhere but with Reid or in my bag, but right now I have to be sure it's there.

CHAPTER FIFTY-THREE

I AM POSITIVE THE PASSENGER MANIFEST IS IN MY LOCKER.

CHAPTER FIFTY-FOUR

The next morning Reid and I approach my locker with cool and calm attitudes, like this is *CSI: Edendale High.* I spin the dial to 23, then 17, and all the way around to 13. The lock clicks open just as it should.

The Passenger Manifest isn't sitting on top, but I decide that means nothing. I hand each textbook to Reid like a pro. Before long, the locker is empty and Reid is holding a stack of books and folders that tower almost past his head.

The Passenger Manifest is nowhere to be found.

"It's lost," I say. "It's officially lost, Reid."

Reid's face, at least what I can see of it, turns the palest shade of white, and the books spill out from his arms onto the floor in all directions. Ted rounds the corner and notices, which I'd normally love. But this is not the time for Ted's help.

"Hi, Riley," he says. "Hey," he says to Reid.

"Ri." Reid is in serious business mode. "We have a situation to deal with."

Ted is scrambling around picking up my books and folders. I wish I could enjoy his being gentlemanly.

"Ri!"

"Sorry, yes, I know, Reid." I take my stuff from Ted and give him a smile I hope explains it all except not because he cannot know what's going on. "Hey, we have to deal with this Gold Diggers thing, so I'll see you in history class."

"Okay." He gives me a smile I hope Reid doesn't notice. Not that Ted and I can't smile at each other, but I'm afraid we don't look casual. I'm afraid we're blasting True Love to the universe, and until Milo is officially in my past, I can't blast anything to anyone. "See you, Riley."

I watch Ted walk away, and when I look back to Reid, I have a feeling he did notice. The whole world's painted with signs pointing to Ted and me and our insane happiness with each other—or at least that we've seen each other naked.

"What's with that?" Reid stares at me. "I thought you said you didn't know how things were going with him, and that's why you're still with Milo. It seems like things are going fine. And considering you apparently don't even like kissing Mi—"

"*THE BOOK IS GONE*," I say. "Can we not talk about guys right now?"

The first bell rings, and we stare at each other. We might be Rock Stars but we are not truants.

"See you at lunch," I say. "We'll figure out where it is, right?"

"Yes," he says, but he is not smug Reid or calm Reid or any of the Reids I feel safe and solid around.

In class I try to pay attention, but instead I unzip every section of my purse and backpack, even the ones that are barely big enough for my lip balm.

"Are you okay?" Garrick asks me.

"I'm fine," I say in a way no one would believe. The Passenger Manifest is missing, and I have to accept that. I have to accept someone knows I messed around a lot with Garrick. Someone knows Garrick and Sydney had sex, even though I was sworn to secrecy over that. Someone knows even once I was falling hardcore with Ted I was afraid to end things with Milo because everything about him was so perfect and straightforward.

Reid sits with Madison at lunch, so we can't discuss *THIS GIANT TRAGEDY*. I don't feel like sitting with Lucy and Nathan, and I don't think it's the day to start sitting with Ted at his table. So I go to the library and listen to Andrew Mothereffing Jackson on my iPod and hope the Passenger Manifest magically appears.

It doesn't.

I have Yearbook after school, which I can't skip, even though Reid texts me three times in seventh period to do so. I don't want to slack off on my only extracurricular responsibility, but also I want to sit next to Ted and sneak him secret looks. Ted gives me a Batman Pez dispenser, which I make talk to him instead of paying much attention to our adviser, Ms. Balsavias. Ted is such a responsible student and person, but he has to cover his mouth, and there are tears in his eyes after the third time I make Pez Batman say, "*ALFRED, THERE'S CANDY IN MY NECK.*"

"What are you doing now?" Ted asks me as we're heading outside.

"I can give you a ride if you want, but I have to go deal with a band thing," I say, because Reid texted me from the Coffee Bean & Tea Leaf on Hillhurst, where he's waiting to talk to me. "I'm sorry, I would totally rather hang out with you."

"Band things are important," he says.

And it's okay because we still get a little making out in before I drive him to his mom's office. I do my best to fix my hair and unsmudge my lip balm so I don't look like I've been doing exactly what I've been doing. When I get to the Coffee Bean, I spy Reid on the patio, but I go in to get a hot cocoa first.

"This is *bad*, Ri," Reid says as I walk out and join him.

"I know, Reid, I know." I exhale as I think of something wonderful. "At least the big stuff isn't in there."

Reid's eyebrows knit together. "What do you mean, 'the big stuff'?"

Oh, *crap.*

I cover my face with my hands. "I, um, Ted and I are, like, actually kind of serious, I guess, and we...kind of did it."

"*'Kind of'*?" His voice has gone all pinched. "What does 'kind of' mean?"

"It doesn't mean anything," I say. "We did it." (I don't say "three times.") "I didn't want to make it sound like a big deal."

"It's a big deal." Reid is mussing his hair all about. The

264

static building in it seems like it's coming from inside, like electrical anger. "I can't believe this. What's the point of the Passenger Manifest if you leave something like that out?"

"It was *private*." Then I hate myself because is that why Lucy never said anything about Nathan? Am I hurting Reid as bad as Lucy hurt me? Am I somehow worse, though, because Lucy never specifically made a pact with me to tell me everything?

"I shared private stuff with you," Reid says. "You know that."

Tears are pricking my eyes, but I am determined not to have an outburst of emotion on the Coffee Bean & Tea Leaf patio. "Reid, I know. But you should understand that's something you don't just want to write about."

"How would I?" Now it's Reid whose face is hidden behind his hands. "Just great, everyone but me is—"

"It's not like we thought," I say. "Just—everything's the same. You know?"

"No," Reid says. "I don't know. The Passenger Manifest is gone, we don't know who has it and what they're going to do with it or try to get out of us for blackmail, and I'm not going to be *relieved* that you having sex didn't make it into the pages. Me never having sex definitely is all over that book."

"At least you got to second-and-a-half base?"

"Shut up, Ri."

It puts me way closer to crying.

"I'll call you or email or something."

"Okay," I say. "Reid, I'm—"

"Whatever."

He walks off, so I sit there and finish my hot cocoa and try not to cry. I would text Ted but he's interning, and also I feel strange going to Ted for comfort when a bunch of this is about him.

All of this makes me want to barf, so I toss out my half-empty cocoa and head out. At home Ashley and her friends are making too much noise in the living room while Dad grades tests in the kitchen, so I escape to the guesthouse. I try to bang out every horrible fear that's in me, but I don't feel any better.

*   *   *

"I have a plan," Reid says, barely looking at me. He came over after dinner but I know that doesn't mean we're already okay. "Let's just be honest with everyone."

I'm not sure if this is his real plan or if he's just trying to make use of dramatic irony. "What do you mean?"

"I'm going to tell Madison what's in there," he says, looking sure of himself. "And Jane and Jennie and Erika."

I miss this Reid, actually.

"If we tell everyone involved what's in there, nothing worse can happen, right?" he asks.

Reid has a good point. One day of walking through school waiting for this mystery villain to appear was more than enough. I'm ready for whatever's next.

CHAPTER FIFTY-FIVE

The Passenger Manifest is officially gone, and my life as I
know it is probably over forever.

CHAPTER FIFTY-SIX

When I think about it, the easiest person to tell about the Passenger Manifest is Garrick.

We've already officially ended things, and anything I wrote about him was exceptionally complimentary. Okay, he did tell me not to mention that he had sex with Sydney—and I did—but besides that I doubt he'll be *too* upset.

"Hi, Riley." Garrick opens his door after school. "Syd is over, but you said you needed to talk, so...we can sit out here."

"Oh, okay." I take a seat on the front steps. I want to peek through the windows to see if I can spot Sydney Jacobs being adorable, but that'd be creepy.

I outline the gist of the Passenger Manifest to Garrick. He blinks in surprise a few times, but he nods and keeps listening.

"So there's definitely stuff about you in it," I continue. "Mostly that you're freaking awesome at everything to do with making out."

Garrick grins, but kind of like that's old news. "Thanks."

"It probably sucks for you that whoever has it knows that happened."

He raises his eyebrows. "Why would that suck for me?"

"Just, you know, Sydney's...and I'm..."

"My therapist said this would happen!"

"What did she say would happen?" I ask. "A weird stupid girl would write about you in a notebook?"

"You're not weird and stupid," he says. "Well, you're not stupid. She said—it might not be easy for people—for girls to know I went out with Syd." He shrugs. "Because, you know."

"She's beautiful and talented and perfect?"

"Famous is what I was going to say! You're beautiful and talented, too, and she isn't perfect." *GARRICK IS SO NICE.* "For a while I hoped something would happen with you. I just can't help how I feel about Syd."

"Trust me," I say, "I understand. I'm totally falling in love with someone, too."

"Thanks for telling me about the book," he says. "But it's okay."

"I should say the rest of it. I wrote about that you did it with Sydney in the book, and I know you swore me to secrecy, but..."

He sighs. "I really hope that doesn't get out, just because she worries about her reputation and stuff, since her fans are so young and their parents get weird about stuff—but, okay. Fine."

"Are you mad?" I ask. "You can hate me if you want."

270

"I don't hate you," he says. "It sucks, and I don't get why you did this whole thing. But in chemistry you always forget to take down full notes when we're doing experiments. I'm impressed you managed on this."

"You can quit being my chemistry partner if you need to."

"I have fun with you," he says. "Though you *should* take better notes. And never do something like this again."

"I promise I won't." I don't say anything about taking better notes because that seems like more of a distant dream.

"Also can I guess who you're in love with?"

"If you want," I say, my heart pounding like my bass drum.

"Ted Callahan?"

"Ted Callahan," I confirm.

"That guy's great," he says. "I'm glad it's someone great."

OH MY GOD, GARRICK IS SO AMAZING.

I give him a huge hug, and he asks me if I want to go inside and meet Sydney. I do, but I act cool about it and say I'll meet her soon and I'm happy for him.

Also I'm going to make my hair look better before I meet Sydney Jacobs.

I get into my car, and it's like the world is reborn and flowers have sprouted up everywhere, and I can breathe again because I start thinking about it, and maybe Milo will be even easier to tell. He doesn't go to my school, he doesn't know any of my friends, and I said lots of things about him being the perfect guy.

I know technically I could definitely get away with not

even telling him. It must be someone at school who has the notebook, and I never used Milo's last name, so they'd never be able to track him down. But this weird part of me doesn't even dread telling him the truth about Ted. That part thinks it'll be good to finally say what's what and move on.

* * *

Milo is free, so I drive over to his house for the first time. It's two stories and huge and there's a basketball court in the driveway and a beautiful seasonal wreath on the front door. When I ring the doorbell, it plays soothing chimes.

"Hey." Milo opens the door. "Come on in."

"Something kind of bad happened," I blurt out.

"What do you mean?" Milo asks. "Are you okay?"

"Okay, so, me and my friend Reid—well, let me back up, a while back, we found out my other two bandmates were doing it, and—basically, I didn't have much experience with guys and Reid had zero experience with girls, and we were like, if Lucy and Nathan are always off doing it, maybe we should be off living, too."

"So you did it with Reid?" Milo shrugs. "That's not a big deal."

"No, ew, I did *not* do it with Reid. We, um, we teamed up to help each other find love or sex or whatever. And we kept track of everything in a notebook. *IS THAT THE WEIRDEST?*"

"Well, yeah, a little?" Milo kind of laughs. "So you wrote about me in it? Is this what you're telling me?"

"Yes," I say. "The notebook's missing, and I'm sure it's someone at my school, and there's really no way it could get back to you, but I wanted to be honest. I wrote about you, and also I was seeing other guys at the same time."

"Well, we weren't exclusive," he says, which is so right and true, I want to high-five him. "But I wish you would have said something. I guess I think you *should* have said something."

"Yeah, I know," I say. I want to end it there, but I know I have to keep going. "AlsoIthinkI'mfallinginlovewithsomeone, so..."

"Oh." Milo stares down at the ground. "And it's not me, I'm guessing."

"We can still hang out," I say. I should have realized this a while ago, and I definitely should have said all of this way sooner than now. "If you even want to. I like going to shows with you, and—and you're awesome! I just...don't want to go out with you anymore. Is that okay?"

He shrugs. "I guess it has to be."

"The part about us hanging out, not about not going out anymore."

Milo sighs really loudly. "I should have probably known something was up. You were always avoiding doing stuff."

"I'm sorry you noticed," I say, even though even Reid figured that out just from the Passenger Manifest. "I should have been more honest. Well, honest, period."

I give him a hug, which he semi-accepts, but then he says he'll hopefully see me at the Diarrhea Planet show in three weeks, so I think we'll be okay as friends or at least as fellow show-goers. And Garrick and I will be fine, too! He is in love with Sydney Jacobs! And I am in love with Ted, and if things are going so easily, I can totally stay in love with Ted.

I call Reid once I'm in my car. "Hey. Your idea was good."

"What idea?" he asks.

"The whole honesty thing," I say. "It was hard, but...eventually Milo and Garrick were both supercool about it, and now I just have to talk to Ted."

"I'm working up the nerve to call everyone," he says. "But it went fine?"

"Yeah, they weren't that mad, and I'm staying friends with both of them."

"Cool." He sounds like the Reid I know and platonically love. "I'll give you an update later. Tell me how it goes with Ted. Or if you hear anything from anyone about the book."

"Will do." I end the call so I can call Ted. "Hey, is this an okay time? Are you busy at your mom's work?"

"It's an okay time," Ted says.

"Can we meet up? I need to talk to you about something."

"Can you come over here? I can meet you outside my mom's office."

I get nervous when I text him to come down, but I tell myself to calm the heck down. Talking to Ted is going to be *fine.* Especially because when he walks up, he's smiling like I have brought all the sunshine back into his world.

"Hi, Riley," he says.

"Hey." I forget why we're here, and I hug him, and even though we're kind of in public—well, totally in public—I kiss him. He laughs nervously, but he kisses me back.

"What's up?" Ted takes a bag of M&M's out of his pocket and passes it to me.

"Um, so this is stupid, and it's really not a big deal, but it could come up, so I want you to know," I say. "So, like, Reid and I, we kept this book, it's just this idea we had back when we found out Lucy and Nathan were together. We figured it didn't make any sense for us not to have any experience, and since we weren't interested in each other, we were helping each other, like, succeed with people they were interested in—"

"What do you mean, 'succeed'?" Ted asks.

"You know, fall in love or do it or whatever." Even though I've already said it twice it sounds worse out loud this third time. Ted confirms this by giving me a look like I'm covered in bees and bad ideas. "It wasn't as awful as it sounds, I swear."

"So you were trying to 'succeed' with me?" he asks.

"No, well, yes, but—I had the biggest crush on you." Now I'm embarrassed for admitting that. Except *WE HAVE DONE IT THREE TIMES.* I shouldn't be embarrassed by that. I don't want to be scared of just saying honest things. "So, like, in a sense. Yeah."

"And you kept track of it like a project?" Ted starts pacing around in a circle and it's making me dizzy, so I try to stop him but he keeps going. "And you let Reid read it?"

"I *had* to," I say. "We made a pact. Except I never told him about...like, recent stuff. None of that's in there."

Ted shakes his head and finally stops pacing. "It's weird, Riley."

"I know, completely, yes, right, ugh!" I feel whatever was spinning out of control settling back, and I'm determined to keep it all right here where it still feels scary and unsure but not unfixable. "I was trying so hard to figure out how to, I don't know, make you like me. It's dumb, and I know it's dumb, and, seriously, once you started meaning something to me I stopped."

Ted nods. "Okay."

"Are you mad?"

"I don't know what I am," he says.

"I should say, also, just a couple other things," I continue, even though I could just stop and maybe things could all be fine. Hopefully they'll be fine anyway. "One, I was seeing some other guys, not like in a big-deal way, but I was. Also I wrote about them in the book, too, and now someone stole the book, so probably everyone at school is going to hear about all of this."

"How many other guys?" Ted asks.

"Just two." I immediately regret that *just*. Right now there is clearly no *just two* to Ted. Two is suddenly a big number.

"Okay." Ted backs away from me. "I'm...I'm going home."

"I can give you a ride," I say.

"No," he says.

"Ted, are you pissed?" I ask, even though of course he is.

"I don't know, Riley, you kept some kind of secret log book with Reid Goodwin, you went out with other guys when I thought you were my girlfriend, and now the whole school's going to know it."

"You thought I was your girlfriend?" I can't stop the question nor the eager tone I ask it in. Riley, shut up.

He starts walking away.

"Don't *do* that!" I run after him, even though Ted is fast on foot. "Ted, don't just say *nothing*."

But he does exactly that. Even though I've managed to catch up with him, he's completely silent.

"I know it was dumb, okay?" I realize that I'm mad and that I shouldn't be and that makes me madder. I hate emotions. "Can we just talk?"

But his answer must be no, because he just keeps walking. His hair is getting longer, and I think about all the times recently I have run my fingers through it, and how maybe this means I never will again. And I am madder still, at everyone in the world about this, Reid, and the notebook thief, and Lucy and Nathan, and Garrick and Milo *FOR MAKING IT SEEM SO EASY*, and Ted, and of course myself.

"Go get your stupid hair cut!" I yell at him, which is the

dumbest because I don't even want him to, I just want his hair less appealing if I have no access to it. Also I'm just the worst right now and I know it, and I'm glad that's the last thing I can say because by now Ted is far away from me.

I get in my car, but I don't go anywhere because there's no way I can see through the ten billion tears I'm crying.

I've ruined everything.

CHAPTER FIFTY-SEVEN

It's still gone, and if it wasn't, I would destroy it.

CHAPTER FIFTY-EIGHT

I spend my whole night crying and risk the wrath of the United Front by refusing dinner as well as not leaving my room at all. I keep my phone near me at all times, but it doesn't ring or beep. The only email I get is from Nathan, reminding us that practice will be long again on Thursday because we need to get ready for our show. Thanks for telling us, Nathan; we'd have no idea without you.

At school the next morning there's no one whispering about me, so I guess this villain is keeping the book under wraps for whatever they're planning. For some stupid reason I check my locker like maybe Ted's over being mad at me so he's left me a CD or candy or a note, but he hasn't left me anything. He walks by me when I'm headed to first period, and I don't know what to do—like, do I look away or do I look sad or do I say something? But I don't have a chance to do any of those things because he darts away from me.

Garrick smiles when I walk into chemistry, and I'm glad at least one person doesn't hate me. "Hi, Riley."

I try to sit at our station like a normal person, but I put my face down on the lab table.

"Hey, Riley, don't do that. I don't trust the janitor to clean up chemicals with proper protocol," Garrick says. "Are you okay?"

I shake my head. "Ted hates me."

"People can get mad," he says, "and then they can get over it."

Garrick is right about everything to do with science, but I don't believe him on this.

* * *

Reid intercepts me on my way to lunch. "Ri, we need to talk *now*. Come on."

I follow him down the hallway to the library. I wait for him to bring up my red and puffy eyes or the fact that I'm wearing a pajama shirt with jeans or any other *SIGNIFICANT SIGN* that I am falling apart.

"The honesty thing did not go like you said it would," he says. "Jane is pissed that I lied about wanting a dog—"

"But you have the dog now! And you love him!"

"And Madison says 'second-and-a-half base' is the dumbest thing she's ever heard."

"Reid, oh my god, why would you tell her *THAT* part?"

"Ri, we swore to be honest." He shakes his head so forcefully I worry he's going to sprain something in his face. "Jennie and Erika didn't really act like they cared, but I'm sure they think I'm a creep."

"Reid, I'm—"

"I can't believe I let you talk me into this."

"Talk you into *what?* Being honest was your idea!"

"The Passenger Manifest," he says.

"Are you serious? That was *both* of our ideas. Don't make this about me."

"I wouldn't have done any of this without you."

"Neither one of us would!"

Ms. Jensen, the school librarian, walks over and literally *shush*es us. I don't feel like standing here and getting yelled at by Reid, who's clearly taken up residence in Crazy Town, so I walk out like it's a regular day and I'm going to go eat lunch.

I tell myself not to, but I glance over at Ted's lunch table. He's in between Brendon and Toby, who are gesturing frantically about whatever guys gesture about. I do my best to make eye contact, but instead of returning it, he looks right through me.

* * *

We have practice after school because timing is crappy. I don't want to see Reid, and I don't want to act normal around Lucy and Nathan, and basically everything in the world sucks.

I'm trying to concentrate on "Stop Talking/Start Dancing," but my mind is only sort of with the music. Every time I hear Reid's bass I wish it was a tangible thing I could punch. We finish the song, but unlike how often that's a moment of triumph, the four of us glance around like we're acknowledging it was crappy.

"Let's take that one again," Nathan says. "It could have been a lot cleaner."

"I think something's off with the drumming," Reid says.

"I think something's off with the drumming," I chipmunk at him. "Why don't you go detail it to death in a book?"

Reid stares at me for a moment like he's making sure he heard what he heard. "Why don't you lie about it and pretend it never happened?"

Lucy's mouth is agape like an extra in a crowd scene from a monster movie.

"Whoa, guys." Nathan looks back and forth between us. "Let's just take it again from the top."

"Let's not." I get up from behind my drums. "You're not President of the Band. And I don't want to do this today. Maybe at all."

The "at all" is a bluff. It just feels so great to say.

"Riley," Lucy says. "Let's go inside and talk."

I don't even respond to her. I leave my drums in the garage and walk out. I've never left them somewhere before, and it's as if I'm leaving my heart and lungs behind. But I drive away like I'm brave.

At home I work on homework because what else am I going to do? Still, everything seems pointless. Who cares if

I can do the quadratic equation if I have no friends and Ted hates me and my band is over?

My phone beeps, and I come up with a billion wonderful possibilities. It's Ted, saying everything's okay! It's Reid, and he's calm and cool and collected and apologetic and wants to go shopping for vinyl, which is boring, but I can live with it! It's Madison, and she's made me more jewelry and boxes to put it in! (That would be surprising. But I'd take it,)

The text *is* from Reid, but it is not about vinyl.

Way to make everything worse.

CHAPTER FIFTY-NINE

No, seriously. Where is the freaking book??

CHAPTER SIXTY

Lucy is sitting on her front porch when I walk up on Friday afternoon to get my drums back. Her hands are wrapped around a mug of cider, and she looks like a postcard for fall. "Hey. Do you want to stay for a while?"

"Sure." I follow her down the hall to her room. Just five months ago if this much of my life was falling apart, I would tell Lucy to tell me what to do, so maybe I should do that now. And Lucy won't think my guy problems are silly and childish, because now we've both done it.

Except, wait, it's not like I think Reid's girl problems are silly and childish just because he's holding steady at second-and-a-half base. Which means maybe Lucy never would have— no. I am not doing this now. I am getting advice and fixing stuff.

"Hey, um." I keep getting distracted looking around her room for ch-ch-ch-changes, but it's all but identical to last time I was in here. I'm happy the framed Jonestown documentary poster I bought her for her last birthday is still in its very prominent place over her desk.

"I'm glad you came over," she says, which feels dangerously close to saying something about, uh, *EVERYTHING*, so I get ready to launch into my crap because, Lucy, let's not do this. Lucy, don't make a big deal over any of it.

"I need advice," I say. "I had all this stuff happen, and it was bad, maybe, I don't even know, but I have to talk to someone about it, and Reid is pissed at me and—"

"So because Reid won't talk to you, I'm good enough to talk to again?" Lucy says it in such a sweet, calm manner I don't even take it the way I should at first.

"I never thought you weren't good enough to talk to," I say, because that's crazy. Lucy, that's crazy! "You were the one—"

"I was the one who what?" She stares at me, very direct eye contact, and I break away because it's horrible.

"You didn't tell me *anything*," I say.

"No," she says. "I didn't tell you that Nathan and I were going out. That was *it*. And it's not like you've told me anything that's going on with you lately."

I guess I always knew she knew that I cut her off. So I'm not expecting to feel worse hearing it.

But my heart pounds and my stomach tightens and this is definitely worse.

"We've been best friends for almost ten years, Riley. I can't believe you let *a boy* come between us."

"It wasn't like that! It's because you never told me, and if we didn't walk in on you guys, maybe you never would have."

"I would have," she says quickly. "Eventually."

"It made me feel so bad," I say. "Like I meant nothing to you and didn't deserve to know anything actually important."

"You should have just said you felt like that before," she says. "Instead of hating me forever."

"I'm sorry," I say. "I was a jerk. And I get it now. Like, sometimes you just need something to be for yourself only. And not because other people don't deserve to know, just…stuff's private."

"For me it wasn't even that!" she says. "I was just sorting out this big new thing, and I was afraid to let it out of my head. I kept imagining how I'd tell you, and you would point out the reasons it was a bad idea—and I knew all those reasons! So I thought, okay, I'll figure out what I want to do first, and then it'll make sense, and Riley will get it and be happy for me."

"I'm happy for you," I say. "Sorry it took me so freaking long."

"Eh, don't be now," she says. "Nathan and I broke up. A couple of weeks ago, actually."

"What? Why? When? Wait, you said when. Why? What? Really?"

"Really." She doesn't answer my other questions. I don't blame her. I'm so annoying sometimes.

"I couldn't even tell!" I say like I just tried I Can't Believe It's Not Butter! and can't believe it's not butter. "Sorry, just, I couldn't."

"We don't hate each other or anything, it's just…" She rolls her eyes. "Nathan's kind of annoying and bossy."

"Duh," I say.

"Shut up, I know! He's also really cute."

"Duh," I say again, and she laughs. "I'm seriously really sorry, Lucy. I've missed you so much."

Her smile fades, and I wonder if I've finally said too much somehow.

"Hang on," she says. She jumps up to root around on her desk, and when she turns around, something is in her hands.

The Passenger Manifest is in her hands.

THE PASSENGER MANIFEST IS IN HER HANDS.

"Here." She sets it in my lap. "I found it in the garage after practice the other week."

"Oh my god." I try to think of something to say, to explain, to make this way less horrifying. *"OH MY GOD."*

I hope that however she responds makes things less awkward, but she doesn't say anything.

"Did you tell anyone?" I ask.

"No."

I flip through the book like it's new, and I'm reading it through Lucy's eyes. It's a terrible experience, so I quit pretty quickly and shove it into my bag.

"I should have told you I had it," she says. "Right away. I'm sorry, Riley."

I'm not expecting her to apologize. I accidentally just stare at her.

"It's just been so long," she continues. "I know I hurt your feelings by not telling you about Nathan, but...it was like it was so easy for you to cut me off."

"It wasn't easy at all." I ram my hands into my eyes like I

can hide that I'm getting a little emotional having this conversation. "It was the worst."

"You and Reid had all these..."

I expect her to say something about what creeps we are.

"...adventures! You told him *everything*."

I accidentally laugh. "Not everything, trust me."

"More than you told me. I missed you so much," she says. "I needed you to talk to *all the time*."

"I was *SO STUPID*. I thought because you and Nathan were doing it, you'd think I was lame and immature and my boy problems were pathetic. I mean, my boy problems *were* pathetic, but still."

"God," she says, "doing it is not exactly the person-changing event you think it is. It's just one thing that happens."

"No, totally, I know what you mean," I say. "Now I do. Then I was stupid and unfair. And I'm sorry. I missed you so much, too."

Lucy grins. "Do you know what I mean because something happened? Or did you just become wise and mature?"

"Ugh, yes. Something happened, but I don't want to talk about it. I'm all heartbroken now, and I'll just sound emo and start applying eyeliner or something."

"Anything but that." She sips her cider. "You can talk about it, though, really. The heartbroken emo part if you want, or just the good parts."

Ted still hates me, and I am probably doomed to a guy-free, kiss-free, doing-it-free life, but I already Just Know that the Gold Diggers are back together and opening for Murphy-Gomez at the Smell next week. I'd gotten used to feeling like some evil hand was clenching my heart and lungs and pushing down on my shoulders all the time, but right now I am sitting up straight and tall and feeling completely like myself.

"I'll tell you all the parts," I say. "But I should warn you that a lot of it is insanely stupid."

"Yay! I love insanely stupid!"

"So there was this guy—" I stop myself. "Well, you know there were guys. But, specifically, there was Ted Callahan."

"I *knew* it," she says. "Even before I read your book. Especially once he showed up at the Andrew Mothereffing Jackson show."

"Don't get excited! He hates me now."

I tell her the whole story. It takes forever because I include all the details I didn't see fit for the Passenger Manifest. I finally break down and demand my own mug of cider. We play a Beach Fossils album while Foley the cat purrs on the bed next to us, and it's like old days. I'm crying by the time I'm finished talking. It's not that I screwed up and made Ted rightfully hate me—well, it's that, but it's more that I had, like, a perfect life. I had amazing friends and a kick-ass band, and then I fell for a guy who fell for me. And I'd been dwelling a lot on the sad parts, but right now I'm flooded with memories of getting candy from Ted and going to shows with Ted and being all tangled together in bed with Ted.

And I miss all of it.

"Well," Lucy says once the talking is over and most of the crying is, too, "there's only one way I know how to deal when I'm sad or I messed up."

"Read about cults?"

"Okay, two things! No, I write songs."

"Ugh, you know I can't write songs! It's one of my failings in life."

"No, I have an idea," she says, her eyes getting anime-round, the way they do when she's excited about something. It hits me that I haven't seen her look this way in a long time. "I'll write a song for you for him. And we can play it at our show, and you can tell him to be there."

"There's no way he'll come," I say.

"Let's worry about that later." She grabs her notepad off her desk. "Okay, tell me what you'd say to him if you could."

"It's weird," I say. "Like, it's a song from you to him."

"It won't seem like it. I'll make it sound like you're the one writing it."

"You can do that?"

"Riley, yes!" She flings her pen at me and gets another off her desk. "I'm a writer! Not every song I write is about me!"

I had no idea. This might make me an idiot. But I trust Lucy. So I tell her everything.

*　*　*

I'm still mad at Reid, and I know he's still mad at me, but he deserves to know. I text him once I'm home from Lucy's.

fyi lucy had the book. it must have fallen out at practice. i got it back.

He responds immediately. Thanks. And, crap.

Okay, he doesn't sound superfriendly, but we're talking again. Well, we're "talking" again. And that's much better than I expected today.

* * *

Reid marches right up to me at school on Monday morning. "Where is it?"

"At home in my nightstand drawer," I say. "What should we do with it?"

"Burn it? My therapist says it should be symbolic." He shrugs. "My mom made me start therapy after I told her everything."

"YOU TOLD YOUR MOM EVERYTHING?"

"Yeah, my therapist says that's weird, too."

It feels sort of normal, I realize.

"Everything got really stupid," I say.

"I know. Sorry I blamed you."

"Sorry I lied to you."

Since we're not huggers, we nod at each other. It feels like a hug!

"There's a cute receptionist at my therapist's office," Reid says, and I laugh really hard.

"I missed you so much." It's not the kind of thing I'm used to saying to him, but he doesn't give me a look like I've gone Hallmark card sentimental on him.

"Yeah, Ri, you too."

CHAPTER SIXTY-ONE

Reid and I buy a big metal trash can and lighter fluid, and we play CeeLo's "Fuck You" through my iPod over Reid's portable speakers, and we totally burn the book. Then we high-five and go out for waffles.

CHAPTER SIXTY-TWO

Within a few days, the plan has been made for me—literally, Lucy has told me what I have to do—but instead of approaching Ted, I stare at him from behind my open locker door.

"Does he look heartbroken?" I ask. "Like that he could cry?"

"He looks how he always looks," Lucy says. "Just go over."

"He looks a *little* heartbroken," Reid says, and I punch his arm.

"He always looks like that," Nathan says.

I punch him, too. Nathan's a lot stronger than Reid, so it's less satisfying, except for that I have long dreamed of punching Nathan. We didn't officially make up or talk, but it turns out Nathan and I can just kind of get along when it's called for.

"Seriously, I can't believe you're stressing over *that guy*," Nathan says.

"I am in love with that guy," I say. "And he deserves better than me."

"Don't wimp out now," Lucy says sternly.

Ted has to walk past us, and Lucy takes that opportunity to *LITERALLY SHOVE ME* in his direction. I smile at him, but he doesn't respond in any manner, so I turn back to look at Lucy.

Follow the plan! she mouths.

"Hi," I try. Step 1!

"Hi, Riley," he says.

It worked!

"I, um, I wrote you a note," I say. Step 2! "I know you might not want to read it, and you totally have every right. But I wanted to explain some stuff, so, anyway."

I take it out of my pocket and hold it out toward him. Step 3! If he doesn't take it, I promise myself very sternly I will gracefully walk away. (Step 4A!)

But Ted looks right at me and takes the note. (Step 4B!) "Okay."

"Okay, I'm going to..." I kind of back away from him, and I turn once it seems like I'm walking backward for a weird length of time. "Bye, Ted."

He doesn't say anything, so I keep walking down the hallway. But at last I hear it, very softly, mixed in with the noise of the school: "Bye, Riley."

CHAPTER SIXTY-THREE

Dear Ted,

I'm seriously so sorry for being such a liar and a weirdo. I wish I could take back all of it, but that would involve magic or time travel and I have access to neither.

Earlier this year I was so scared of losing my friends and my band, and I made some stupid decisions. I liked you before then, and then you just kind of got roped into this whole plan of mine and Reid's.

You're seriously the smartest, nicest, funniest guy I have ever met. I love your mix CD ability and your messenger bag. I like how when we talk I feel like I'm the most important person ever. I think it's super kick-ass that you run the Fencing Club, and do you remember the time I called it the Fenching Club? It was only because I was so nervous to be around you because I had the biggest crush in the world on you, and I couldn't function normally.

I want to be upfront and say I really want to get back together with you. I know I lied and hurt you, and I can't take that back. I screwed up. I'm seriously so sorry, Ted—not just because I lost you but because I don't want to be a bad person.

The Gold Diggers are playing at the Smell on Saturday night. There's going to be a special song for you, so I hope you will come hear it. And if you don't, I will understand.

Love+apologies+everything,
Riley

CHAPTER SIXTY-FOUR

We're crowded into the Smell's tiny greenroom staring at our set list and making sure we look as cool as possible. I wish Reid wasn't wearing *A BLAZER* and I can tell from Lucy's expression she agrees, but I guess this is his thing now.

"We should look out to see if he's here," Reid says.

"I would bet he isn't," Nathan says.

"Nathan, come on," Lucy says.

"Not because of Riley breaking his heart. Just, I can't imagine that guy here."

"He's pretty rock-and-roll," Lucy says. "He was fun at the Andrew Mothereffing Jackson show, remember? He'll come."

"YOU GUYS ARE WAY TOO INVESTED IN THIS," I say in a voice I meant to be calm. *"CAN WE FOCUS ON WHAT'S IMPORTANT, PLEASE."*

"He'll come," Lucy says again.

"This set list is solid," Nathan says. *El presidente* rises again! "And I didn't want to freak you guys out, but—well, we're in this together. I'll just tell you. My cousin helped me get in touch with this guy, and he's coming tonight, and if he likes us, he'll think about managing us."

We stare at him, and I want to yell at him for springing this on us, but I know for Nathan this is the best he can do, and I get it. Also we are going to have a great show, and this dude is going to love us. At this very moment it seems possible, and not just because right now almost anything seems more probable than my—well, *Lucy's*—plan actually working.

The club's getting loud, and when we walk onstage, it's like our dreams are coming true, but also we earned this. We've worked so hard and somehow didn't kill each other, and standing here in a place I love makes a whole lot of sense.

We open with "Tease," and even though I'm sure 90 percent of the crowd is here to see Murphy-Gomez, people are jumping around and dancing and acting exactly how people should act at a show. We roll right into "Longer Days," and then Nathan introduces us and thanks the crowd for being there. But then he gives Lucy a chance to talk, too! Nathan is clearly becoming a better person, or at least pretending, which is good enough for me.

It's a shorter set than we had at the dance, but we manage to get in a bunch of originals, plus our pretty fantastic (if I'm handing us compliments) cover of Andrew Mothereffing Jackson's "Never Gonna (Love Me)." After that I don't need to look at my set list to know what's next, but I still quadruple check it to see it's going to happen *AND I DON'T EVEN KNOW IF TED'S HERE TO HEAR IT.* But it's okay because Lucy wrote an amazing song that sounds like it's from me and not her, and I'm glad we're playing it.

About that time I called you names
Or that other time when we were playing games
I know I'm young and kind of insecure
But that was dumb; I was in the wrong for sure

No, I don't think that you should cut your hair
I like the way you always seem to care
About the world; oh hell, what do I know
I'm just a girl, a girl who wants to show you

Everything I could ever offer
Everything that you could ever want
Everything you could ever dream of
I want to show you everything

About that time I almost caused a scene
Or that other time you fed me jelly beans
I never thought that this would ever grow
I never believed that I would get to show you

Everything I could ever offer
Everything that you could ever want
Everything you could ever dream of
I want to show you everything

The reason that I couldn't let you see
All the good and bad and ugly of me
The reason that I didn't think this was real
Is you're the only one who's ever made me feel

About that time when we were in my car
Or that other time we kissed under the stars
Or that other time... we didn't make a sound

I want to show you
Everything I could ever offer
Everything that you could ever want
Everything you could ever dream of
I want to show you
I want to know you
I want to be your
Everything

After our set, I focus on packing up my drums as quickly as I can while hanging on to how the crowd screamed for us. We are Rock Stars. We did something big and right. I just want to enjoy this.

A small man with Elvis Costello hair and glasses walks over to us as we leave our stuff backstage and emerge into the crowd. This must be Nathan's dude because he's, like, the only adult here besides the owner.

"Hey, guys," he says. "Nice set. Very Best Coast, a little Smith Westerns. You're not signed, yeah?"

I feel like he's complimented us and pointed out our biggest failing all at once.

Nathan introduces us. "This is Melvin Bernstein."

"How about we meet next week to talk?" he asks. "I have Nathan's info. Maybe grab dinner at FOODLAB on Sunset?"

We're down with that, so we each get his business card like professionals and manage to look chill and respectable until he heads off. That only lasts for a few moments because people we know start flying in at us. Both of my sort-of exboyfriends are there, but it's fine. Milo is alone, and Garrick brought Sydney Jacobs. She is as adorable and blond as I imagined she'd be, and dressed better than me, but it makes me happy that she's smiling and Garrick is smiling, and clearly they are the happiest ever. I hug them all, even Madison—who's standing really close to Reid and shooting him looks like he's the biggest rock star of us all—and Sydney, and bask in the warmth of a billion compliments.

"Hey, look who's here." Lucy walks over, her hand clutched around Ted's sleeve. I'm not crazy about the fact that he had to be *LITERALLY PHYSICALLY DRAGGED* to me, but he's here!

"Ted, you're here!" Yikes. I accidentally say this part aloud.

Luckily, Ted laughs. Then he glances at Milo, and I make a face like, *no, gross,* which is not nice to Milo but very necessary in this all-important moment. I'm sure Milo will understand when I tell him later.

"Great show, Riley," Ted says.

"I'm so glad you came." I want to believe it means something big and romantic.

"I, uh, I wanted to say something to you." He gestures a few feet away from everyone, so we separate from the pack.

"I wanted to ask you to be my girlfriend," he says. "But I didn't, I was nervous and . . . so, I'm not saying everything you did was cool, but we weren't official."

"Still," I say. "I wanted to be official. I should have said it, but I was nervous, too."

"Okay," he says. *WAY TO BE VAGUE, TED.*

"So do you want to be?" I ask. "Now that you know I'm a big jerk weirdo?"

"You're not a jerk," he says. "And I already knew you were a weirdo."

I grin at him and lean in to kiss him. *BUT HE DODGES ME.*

"Every single person we know here is watching us," he says. "And some girl who I think is on TV."

I turn around, and they aren't even trying to hide it! We have this huge audience of looky-loos. I'm plotting where we can sneak off to for major making out, but Ted shrugs at me like we may as well just give in. I start to head back to our group.

And he kisses me.

It is not a Ted-style timid kiss; it is a Ted-style big, swoony romantic kiss. It's exactly what I've been dreaming of. I run my hands through his hair, and his fingertips find a gap to graze between my jeans and my shirt I didn't know was there. Ted tastes like a green apple Jolly Rancher.

"I missed you." He whispers it right in my ear, his warm breath almost like another kiss. Okay, not *almost*, but it's hot. "Can you hang out later?"

"Yes, definitely," I tell him. "You don't have to get up early to fry hot dogs?"

"Yeah, but I don't care," he says. Then he takes my hand as we walk back over to our group. From the stage I hear the opening riff of my favorite Murphy-Gomez song, and the crowd starts filling in around us.

Ted smiles at me as I grin back at him, and he leans in to kiss me again. "I really liked your song."

ACKNOWLEDGMENTS

Staying motivated when I first started working on this book was, for a number of boring and depressing reasons, quite difficult. Thank you so much to Nadia Osman for working through scenes with me, writing songs for me, and in general being exactly the friend I needed during this time. I'm glad I could honor your favorite president in this book.

Thanks also to Stephanie Perkins for the insane amount of support, for the mind-bogglingly helpful notes, and for taking my panicky phone calls. Lady, that stuff never went unnoticed.

Thanks to my agent, Kate Schaefer Testerman, for continued awesomeness, three books in!

Thank you times one billion to my editor, Elizabeth Bewley, for the notes, support, and hard work. I laugh now to think this book was in nearly finished shape when it went to you, because through your guidance I ended up someplace far better.

Thanks to the Pams: Gruber for stepping in, and Garfinkel

311

for always being around to assist. A huge thank-you to the whole Poppy/Little, Brown team for always making me feel appreciated and taken care of, and for loving Riley as much as I do.

Thanks to Carrie Harris for drumming help. Thanks to Scott Singer for, as always, the science. Thanks to Todd Martens for major music help. Thanks to Hope Larson for letting me fictionalize her cat. Thanks to Ariel Schrag for naming boys on command.

Thanks to my early readers and note-givers: Sarah Skilton, Courtney Summers, Trish Doller, Meghan Deans, Brandy Colbert, and Jasmine Guillory. A special shout-out goes to Trish and Courtney for the title!

Lastly, of course, thanks to Pat and Mark Spalding for their eternal support.